"*If I sing for this re_____ough money for us to get m____*

"I know. You planned th'_____ reprimand or accusation.

"I reckon I have to admit I did, after I ___ visitin'. I thought, why not take a chance? I knew if the Lord didn't want this to happen for me, it wouldn't. But Archie hadn't been here five minutes before he asked me to sing. That's got to be a sign, doesn't it?"

"I don't know. I admit, I bragged on you mightily. Should have known better than to brag to a record producer."

"That's just it. Archie is the only person who can help us get the store. I don't want to be no big celebrity like the women in the Carter family. I just want to sing long enough for us to save up and buy the store."

"Really?"

"You know me. Archie's talk about riches don't matter to me none. Once we buy that store, all I want is to entertain my family and be Mrs. Gladdie Gordon."

TAMELA HANCOCK MURRAY is an award-winning, best-selling author living in northern Virginia. She and her husband of over twenty years are blessed with two daughters. Their first, an honors student, is attending college at Tamela's alma mater. Their second, a student at a Christian school, keeps them busy with many church activities, including bell choir and youth group. Tamela loves to take mini vacations with her family, and she also enjoys reading and Bible study. www.tamelahancockmurray.com

Books by Tamela Hancock Murray

HEARTSONG PRESENTS

HP213—Picture of Love
HP408—Destinations
HP453—The Elusive Mr. Perfect
HP501—Thrill of the Hunt
HP544—A Light among Shadows
HP568—Loveswept
HP598—More Than Friends
HP616—The Lady and the Cad
HP621—Forever Friends
HP639—Love's Denial
HP663—Journeys
HP687—The Ruse
HP715—Vera's Turn for Love

The Music of Home

Tamela Hancock Murray

Heartsong Presents

With love to my North Carolina cousin, Gayla McGee Briggs. Her light shines for Christ at all times.

A note from the Author:
I love to hear from my readers! You may correspond with me by writing:

Tamela Hancock Murray
Author Relations
PO Box 721
Uhrichsville, OH 44683

ISBN 978-1-59789-010-6

THE MUSIC OF HOME

All scripture quotations are taken from the King James Version of the Bible.

All of the characters and events in this book are fictitious. Any resemblance to actual persons, living or dead, or to actual events is purely coincidental.

Our mission is to publish and distribute inspirational products offering exceptional value and biblical encouragement to the masses.

PRINTED IN THE U.S.A.

one

Singing a mountain ballad, Drusie Fields looked upon the audience at the church social. The meeting hall was filled with people who had known her since she was born. Drusie's friends and family encouraged her love for singing, applauding every time she performed. She played the banjo and sang, recognizing sweetness in her voice.

Drusie wore her favorite Sunday dress, sewn from red and white polka-dotted flour-sack material and fashioned from a store-bought pattern. In such splendor, Drusie felt she could hold her own with any other girl in the room. She surveyed the crowd and noticed most of the women were dressed in clothing they had sewn themselves, although a few wore outfits ordered from the Wish Book.

Only two of the men stood out to her eyes: Pa, who whistled and clapped, and the love of her life, Gladdie Gordon. She didn't have to search long for Gladdie. His manly face, so easy on the eyes, caught her attention. She smiled at him, noticing his dark hair shining in the dim lights. Applauding for all he was worth, he mouthed the title of a well-loved mountain song.

As usual, he had chosen one of her favorites, "This Is Like Heaven to Me." Drusie smiled and nodded. "This next number is dedicated to Gladdie Gordon. I think y'all are familiar with the tune."

On her banjo, Drusie strummed the first notes of the song

5

he requested, and the rest of the band joined her. Approving claps resonated throughout the small wooden structure that served as a church, meeting hall, and schoolhouse for their Appalachian community.

Drusie hit the high notes with ease. Hearing her sister Clara join her in harmony pleased Drusie. Everybody said they looked perfect together on stage, with Drusie's dark locks and pale complexion complementing Clara's lighter hair and sharp features. Drusie sang as though she were performing for Gladdie and Gladdie alone. She couldn't help it. She loved him.

The song ended, and Uncle Martin shouted above roaring applause, "Sing it one more time, Drusie!"

"Again?" she teased. "Why, you're like to wear me plumb out tonight!" Despite her protests, she felt flattered and had every intention of singing for the crowd as long as they asked.

Drusie noticed Aunt Irma and recalled her recent comment that Drusie looked just like her mother. Ma didn't have a streak of gray in her black hair nor a wrinkle on her petite face. Pa said her eyes were still as blue as the day they were married.

Not that Ma did so bad for herself when she married Pa. Years of working hard as a lumberjack hadn't broken his spirit. Both of her parents were wiry and had passed on that build to Drusie and her five sisters. Pa always said he never stood a chance of getting a word in edgewise with all those womenfolk around, but she could tell by the twinkle in his eyes that he liked it that way.

Old Mr. Harper called out, reminding her she remained onstage. "How about singin' 'Amazing Grace'?"

Drusie gave her audience a good-natured nod. Clara nodded in turn, and the band played the chorus before the sisters sang the first verse. The room fell silent as they listened to the hymn of gratitude and repentance.

Drusie figured that would be the last song of the night, but the crowd wanted more. Tired but elated, Drusie was glad when Silas stepped up and played "Flop-Eared Mule," showing off for all he was worth. The crowd clapped in time.

She made her way toward Gladdie, feeling safe in his nearness. He'd shined up his hair with tonic and shaved closely. His arresting features caught the eyes of more than one girl even though everyone in these parts had known him forever. But everyone there also knew that he was hers, and she stood by him, her erect posture demonstrating pride.

He gave her a sideways grin. "You gonna take back to the stage after Silas finishes showin' off?"

"Again? Why, I'm about played out."

"You'll never play out, Drusie. That sweet voice can go on and on. Especially when you're singin' for the Lord."

She drew closer to him and looked him full in the face. "I love singin' for Him, darlin'."

He gave her a kiss on the cheek. "I love you mightily, Drusie Fields. Your devotion to God is one of the reasons I've loved you since we was nothin' but kids."

She smiled shyly. Looking up, Drusie noticed Edna Sue glancing Gladdie's way. She resisted the temptation to narrow her eyes at the girl who wanted to be her rival. From the corner of her eye, Drusie noticed that Gladdie took his glance away from Edna Sue's as soon as their gazes met. "She's a bold one." Drusie swallowed.

"Too bold for me," Gladdie said. "You know you're the only one I have eyes for, Drusie. I wish we could get married today." He took her by the arm. "Come on. Let's us go for a walk in the moonlight."

She peered around the room. "Will anybody miss us?"

"I won't keep you too long."

She acquiesced, glad to be away from the covetous eyes of the other girls. As soon as she and Gladdie left through the side door, Drusie noticed the chill of autumn air. Scents of leftover ham and sugary desserts from the potluck dinner still hung in the hall but faded as they walked away.

Drusie shivered. "Wish I'd've thought to bring my shawl."

Without hesitation, Gladdie whipped off his suit coat and placed it around her shoulders. The warmth of his body and manly scents of laundry soap and shaving tonic clung to the garment, making Drusie feel cozy and secure as they walked along the narrow moonlit path. It wound through a stand of pines, crossed an open meadow, and eventually led to the old Norman place. Abandoned years ago, the house was reputed to be haunted. For as long as Drusie could remember, local boys tested their bravery in exploring the rickety old abode. But on this night, Drusie and Gladdie wouldn't be walking far enough to test their courage.

"I didn't mean for you to give up your coat for me," she objected with a shy smile.

"Sure you did," he teased. "Naw, I'd've given it up for you anyhow."

Feeling guilty, she glanced back at the meeting hall and slowed her pace. "Maybe we should go back inside, lest you catch your death of cold."

"I'm too strong for that." He flexed a bicep.

She giggled and punched his arm too lightly to kill a fly. "Muscles won't help you none against a cold, silly."

"Oh yeah? Then what will?"

"Come to think of it, I don't reckon I rightly know. But Sarah May's studyin' to be a nurse, so maybe I can find out from her." Drusie shook her head. "She's the smart one out of all of us Fields sisters. I cain't imagine doin' somethin' that hard all my life. Havin' to know all about them medical potions and stuff."

"Aw, you're plenty smart. Smart enough for me. Smarter than I need in a wife." He placed a protective arm around her shoulders.

"Stop it, now." She smiled in spite of herself.

"You know, I've almost got enough money saved up to buy that little weddin' band with orange blossoms in Mr. Goode's store."

She gasped. "You do?" Drusie didn't bother to conceal her happiness. Gladdie knew her heart. The ring itself didn't matter. What it symbolized—their forever love—did.

"I sure enough do. Only, I'd better save up right quick like."

"Why?" she managed, even though she was almost scared to ask such a thing.

"Didn't you know? Mr. Goode's been feelin' right poorly lately, and he wants to go live with his daughter in Raleigh."

"Raleigh! A big city like that? Imagine!" Then a thought occurred to her. "But what will we do around here without his store?"

"We won't have to find out if I can help it."

Drusie didn't need to ask him what he meant. Gladdie came from a farming family, a hardscrabble life as far as he was concerned. Gladdie wanted a different way of life for himself and his future wife. A life that was a little easier than coaxing crops from the land. "So you're still of a mind to buy the store."

"More mind than money, sad enough. I was hopin' Mr. Goode could hold off lettin' go of the store for a couple more years. That would've given me longer to save up enough cash to make a down payment, anyway."

"Do you reckon there's anybody else wantin' to buy the store?"

"I reckon not, leastways nobody from around here. Well, except for the Moores. They'd love to own the only dry goods store in Sunshine Holler. If they bought Mr. Goode's place, they'd stamp out the competition."

"If you got ahold of the store, you'd be competition, sure enough. You're good with cipherin' and details. I know you can keep up with the stock, and I don't doubt you could remember to the penny who owes the store how much money."

Gladdie's chest puffed ever so slightly. "I sure could. Pa says I've got a head for that sorta thing."

"That's right. You can do anything, Gladdie." Drusie wasn't flattering her future husband. Her faith in him was sincere.

"Pa says I got the raw talent, but I got to give Mr. Goode credit. I've learned a lot from him by clerkin' at the store." He stopped under a large sycamore tree whose trunk had been carved with many initials over the years. Not so long ago, Gladdie had carved his and Drusie's in a heart. He shuffled his foot in the dirt. "I reckon I'm a silly dreamer. Who'd ever think a boy only a few years outta high school could own his own business, just like that?" He clapped once, punctuating his remark.

"If anybody can, you can." Drusie sighed. "I just wish I had enough money saved up to help you buy the store."

"I know." He leaned against the trunk, and his voice became dreamy. "Then we could get married in a hurry and I could build you a house of your very own."

"I'd like that. But it would still take awhile for us to get settled even then."

"I reckon so." He studied her, love shining in his eyes. Taking her by the hand, he led her farther down the path. "I wish I could buy you the world. Like pretty dresses. You're so sweet, you deserve fine clothes. And I'd love to afford a diamond ring for you, even bigger than the one that lady was wearin' in that picture show we went to see in town last month."

Drusie remembered. In anticipation of celebrating her twentieth birthday, Gladdie had saved up enough money for gas to drive them into town in the Gordons' Model T and pay the nickel admission apiece for them to see the show. Drusie had heard there were talking pictures showing in big cities, but the one they saw was a silent. She couldn't imagine people talking on film. What was wrong with silent pictures?

Drusie thought back to the picture they saw. She enjoyed the complicated story of how a rich man fell in love with a poor woman. After many setbacks and tribulations, the man's family accepted the woman and they lived happily ever after. The woman started out wearing rags that looked worse than a dress Drusie would cut up to make smaller clothes for her nieces. By the time the picture ended, the heroine was wearing fur coats, silk dresses, and big diamond rings. She recalled how the jewels sparkled under the light. Imagine!

"Wouldn't you like to have some pretty clothes and things rich folk have?" Gladdie queried.

She shrugged. "I figure if the good Lord planned for me to live like a rich city woman, He woulda plunked me right in Raleigh. Not here in Sunshine Holler."

They had reached the edge of the meadow. Gladdie turned them around so they could start walking back to church. "Not everybody stays put, though. Remember my cousin Archie?"

She remembered a red-haired youth who'd gone off to make his dreams come true. "The music producer?"

"That's him. Archie ain't got a bad life. He managed to get his education, get outta this here holler, and go on to make good in the city. I wish I had his courage. I reckon that's what I really mean. I wish I was like him in a lot of ways."

"I don't see a thing in the world wrong with admirin' somebody, especially somebody who shares your blood. Why don't you put that admiration to good use? Try developin' courage on your own, and you'll be more like Archie."

"That's a grand idea, Drusie."

"I don't know much about that, but I try to encourage you."

"And everybody else. I think they named this holler after you—Sunshine—because that's what you are."

❧

A few days later, Gladdie knocked on the door of the modest frame house where Drusie lived with her parents and Clara, the only other sister remaining at home. Upon hearing his summoning knock, Drusie set down her basket of clean socks and went to the door.

"Come on in, Gladdie. I was just about to start in on mendin', but that can wait." Drusie was more than happy to have an excuse to delay the hated chore. Her sister Clara didn't mind repairing little rips and holes in clothes so much, but she was already occupied helping Ma with sweeping and scrubbing the kitchen floor, a task Drusie detested even more than darning. To Drusie's way of thinking, the floor needed scrubbing entirely too often. Ma took pride in the house that Pa and his brothers had built years ago, and she insisted that they keep it spotless.

"I know how much you love mendin'," Gladdie teased. "Once we're married, I'll try to be real careful not to get holes in my clothes."

Drusie grinned and peered at the sun, which had begun its descent. "I don't think I'm the only one skippin' out on chores. Ain't it about time for you to milk the cows?" Her glance swept his form. "You sure are dressed for it, in them dungarees."

He laughed. "Sorry. I didn't have time to put on nothin' better. Ma said I could run over here for a minute or two, but not to leave my brothers with all the work. I've got to get right on back as soon as I share my news."

"If your ma let you get away from your chores, whatever you have to say must be important." She tilted her head toward two rockers on the porch. "We'd best sit outside. Ma and Clara are scrubbin', and that means we cain't let in any dirt for a few days."

Gladdie nodded. A gentleman as always, he waited for her to choose a cane-bottomed rocker before he took the one beside it.

"So your news is right important?" Drusie asked.

"It is." Gladdie's eyes were wide, and his tone of voice conveyed his excitement. "Archie's comin' for a visit. We got a letter from him today."

"Your cousin Archie?"

"I don't know no other Archie."

"I suppose not." A feeling of anticipation tugged at her stomach. "Wonder what brings him here. Did he say?"

"Just for a visit. Since I've always been fond of Archie, I was hopin' maybe you could set aside Wednesday afternoon to come over. Plan on stayin' until suppertime, if it's okay with your ma."

"I'm sure that'll be just fine with Ma. I'll make sure to get ahead on my chores before then." She stared at the dirt road winding past the house and breathed in a whiff of clear mountain air tinged with the musky odor of autumn. "I wonder if he'll even remember me. It's been so long since he took off for the city."

"Oh, I'm sure he'll remember you. But you've gotten real grownified since he left. And we weren't engaged back then."

Drusie couldn't help but notice the pride that colored his voice. "I'll be on my best behavior, then. I don't want to disappoint you."

"You never disappoint me." He rose from his seat. "I have to admit, I do want to show you off."

"You do?"

He nodded. "Bring your banjo. I want him to hear how good we can sing and play around these here parts. He's been in the city so long he's probably forgot."

"I don't know. My puny doin's won't sound like nothin' in comparison to a big act in the city."

He drew closer and put his arm around her. "Don't play for him, then. Play for me."

She smiled, lingering in the warmth of his presence. "For you, Gladdie, I'll do anything."

She didn't tell Gladdie at that moment, but a thought had just popped into her mind. A thought he would like very much.

two

On the day of Archie's visit, Drusie and Gladdie sat on the Gordons' porch in rockers. Swaying back and forth, Drusie imagined they looked more like a couple of old folks with too much time on their hands than the young people they were. But she felt grateful for the chance to sit in silence with the one she loved. Drusie had been nervous earlier, but the interlude offered a chance to calm down before Archie Gordon arrived.

Unwilling to let Gladdie know how nervous she felt, Drusie concentrated on the rhythm of swaying. Ever since she'd known the Gordons, these rockers had sat in exactly the same spot on their front porch. They never had been painted, so the bare wood was smooth with wear. Sheltered as they were by the porch overhang, the rockers still displayed the burden of being outdoors since Mr. Gordon made them years ago. Nail heads showed themselves where the arm handles met railings. Every once in a while she rubbed the smooth metal. The presence of the rockers made Drusie feel secure. As long as they remained, so did the Gordons, and the community Drusie called home.

The Gordon house, like the Fields home, offered a pleasing view of the valley. Cool autumn weather had turned the leaves a variety of hues. Drusie enjoyed seeing bright red, shimmering yellow, blazing orange, and deep green leaves.

"Archie sure picked a pretty day to drive up here." With the back of his head resting against his chair, Gladdie looked with a lazy expression toward the valley. He inhaled an exaggerated breath, a sure sign he wanted to enjoy a good dose of crisp mountain air.

"He sure enough did." Without intention, Drusie followed his example. The air refreshed her, and the ordinary topic of the weather put her at ease. "Hope he enjoys the drive. Leaves sure are pretty."

"Sure are." Gladdie peered at the midday sun. "He left Raleigh yesterday. He's supposed to be here soon."

The fact of Archie's imminent arrival struck her. Drusie tapped on the arm of her chair and rocked faster. "It's gettin' late. You reckon he's had trouble?"

"I don't hardly know." Gladdie shrugged. "But if he ain't had trouble, he'll be here soon, just like he promised. He said noon, so I doubt it'll be much after that. Businessmen pride themselves on being prompt, you know."

Almost as soon as the words were out of his mouth, they saw a cloud of dust kick up on the road. A large automobile roared down the drive to the Gordon house.

"What in the world is that?" Drusie leaned forward in her seat.

"You mean, what kind of automobile is he drivin'?"

"Uh-huh. I ain't never seen one that fancy."

"It's an Auburn. You ain't never seen one of them before?" Gladdie teased.

She eyed the Gordons' aged Model T Ford parked in the side yard. The paint had chipped, but the tires were sturdy. Many of their neighbors didn't have transportation anywhere near that good. "I have a feelin' you ain't never seen an Auburn, either. If Archie hadn't written you about his fancy automobile, you wouldn't be able to tell what you were lookin' at. Now you just try to tell me I'm wrong."

Gladdie's ma rushed through the front door, a spoon coated in ham hock grease in hand, wearing her perennial apron and polka-dotted dress. "What's all that ruckus?" She looked to Archie's automobile and answered her own question. "Oh! He's here! And what an automobile that is!"

Gladdie peered at the vehicle. "I admit, I ain't never seen no automobile so light colored before. Kind of reminds me of the ivory pipe Uncle Ned used to have. Remember that, Ma?"

"I sure do. Sent from some friend workin' in Africa. Naruby or some place like that."

"I don't think that's a practical color for a car, considerin' all the dust on the roads," Drusie observed, then regretted speaking aloud. "I'm sorry. Didn't mean no harm. Just blurted without thinkin'."

"You didn't say nothin' I warn't thinkin'," Gladdie consoled her. "But Archie never was known to be practical. Reckon that's why he's so successful in the music business."

Drusie hadn't seen an automobile that wasn't painted black, either. "It may not be practical, but it's right pretty."

"Sure is," Gladdie agreed.

"Sure is," Mrs. Gordon opined.

Archie pulled up to the house and came to a stop so fast that Drusie was afraid its driver might fly right out of the seat, but he remained steady. She figured the beast of a machine was too weighty to flip over no matter if it got up to fifty miles an hour. "I don't reckon he had time to look at the pretty trees what with drivin' like that and all."

Gladdie agreed. "Maybe not. I imagine he's got more important things on his mind."

Archie cut off the engine, then waved at them as he got out of his car. Gladdie and Drusie stood, watching Archie approach. Though nowhere near as handsome as Gladdie, Drusie guessed that his swagger attracted the womenfolk.

Suddenly Drusie felt self-conscious. She smoothed the skirt of her dress, a cotton affair she had sewn herself from patterned flour sacks. She had to wait two months to use up all the flour, but pretty red flowers on a white background had been worth the test of endurance. As soon as the next batch of flour was done, she could sew a shirt for Pa from the striped material of the sack they were using now. Ma had just gotten some white cotton cloth and a good supply of chintz at bulk discount from Mr. Goode's store and had fashioned herself a new Sunday dress, Pa a shirt, Clara a blouse, and Drusie a skirt. At the rate they were going, the whole Fields family would soon be the best dressed at church.

She looked at Archie. When he laid his gaze upon her, his expression brightened. She was glad she had chosen to wear the flowered Sunday dress. She wanted to look her best so Archie would think his cousin's fiancée was a lady.

She tried not to study Archie too hard, lest he think she was being a flirt. She hadn't seen him in a long time—not since he went to Raleigh four years ago to make good in the city. He had changed from the acne-faced teenager she remembered. The trademark red hair remained, but the acne was gone and the face and physique had matured from a boy's to a man's. He was wearing a suit in a cut she'd never seen. The coat had buttons on both sides and came in at the waist. Perhaps that was the style in the city. A fine suit like that certainly set him apart from her friends and neighbors. He'd stick out like a sore thumb even in church. She wondered if men dressed like that in the city all the time. If so, they must be mighty uncomfortable wearing ties and starched shirts like they were always going to worship service.

"Hey, Gladdie! I'd recognize you anywhere." Archie tipped his hat at his aunt and greeted her, as well.

Gladdie approached Archie, and the two men met midway in the front yard. Drusie watched them embrace. She could see even from the distance that they shared a genuine fondness.

"That's a mighty fine automobile you got there!" she heard Gladdie say.

"A new Auburn Phaeton. Eight cylinder."

"She's a beaut." Although Drusie had never known Gladdie to covet anything, the admiration in his eyes for the automobile was obvious.

"She sure is a great little tin can." Archie gazed at the automobile like a miser would look at hoarded gold.

Mrs. Gordon shook her head. "Men and their machines."

Drusie giggled. The sound apparently attracted Archie's attention, because he looked up at her. "Butter and egg fly! What a tomato!" Ignoring Gladdie, Archie headed toward the house. "Is this Drusie Fields?"

Drusie had never been described in terms of an edible item before, but she assumed from Archie's animated expression that the words were complimentary. "It's me." She didn't make a move to go closer, feeling that to do so would be too forward.

He let out a low whistle, which at once made her feel complimented and strangely shy. "You grew up to be a dish. I'm not surprised. Your mama was always pretty. And what about Clara? Is she a looker, too?"

"We look right much alike for sisters, I reckon," Drusie acknowledged. "I think she's prettier than me."

"Then she must be a hot mama."

"Hold your horses, Archie." Gladdie's voice indicated his displeasure. "The Fields girls are respectable, not some floozies you might meet in the city."

"I know it, cuz." Archie tipped his hat. "Didn't mean to offend, Drusie. Or you, either, Aunt Penny. Although I hope you don't mind my saying that you are as beautiful as ever."

Mrs. Gordon swept her glance upon her apron and back to Archie. "Oh, you hush now! I've got to go finish up lunch." She went back into the house, not bothering to catch the screen door like she usually did. Even over the loud *bang* it made as it shut, Drusie heard Mrs. Gordon's giggles.

Drusie felt more shocked than flattered by Archie's bold words directed her way and a bit embarrassed that Mrs. Gordon acted like a schoolgirl, but she decided to be gracious for Gladdie's sake. "With smooth talk like that, Archie, you must be sellin' records left and right."

Archie laughed and leaned against one of the poles—which weren't anything nearly so grand that they could be called columns—that held up the porch covering. "I only speak the truth," Archie observed, still studying her. "Gladdie here tells me you take the roof off the house with your singing."

Drusie wasn't sure how to respond. "I reckon I do sing right loud."

Archie chuckled. "That's not what I mean. I mean, you're quite the canary, according to Gladdie. And from what I remember, you liked to perform. Is that still so?"

"Well, some people tell me I'm right good at singing, but of course, your ma is supposed to tell you that, I reckon." Now that Archie was asking about her singing, Drusie felt even more anxious. She wished she hadn't shown her unease by punctuating every thought with an expression of uncertainty.

"Your ma, huh?" Archie looked at Gladdie. "You say everybody likes her, not just her ma?"

"That's right," Gladdie said. "She's just bein' modest. I wouldn't have it any other way."

"That's just grand. So are you going to perform for me?" Archie asked.

"Perform? I—uh, sure." Drusie's anxiety turned to an excitement she tried not to display. Her plans were falling into place with no effort on her part. First, Gladdie had asked her to bring her banjo, which was no surprise since she was often called upon to entertain company. Archie, visiting from out of town as he was, would be no exception. But Archie wasn't just any company. He was a record producer—owned a recording studio, even. He was the big boss at his business. What he said went. At least that's what Gladdie told her. If she could impress Archie, then maybe she could cut a record and sell enough copies that Gladdie could buy Mr. Goode's store. After that, she'd retire and they could live happily ever after.

"Sure," Gladdie piped up, interrupting Drusie's daydream. "Drusie will play the banjo for you. She'll even sing whatever song you request. If she knows it, that is. And she knows plenty of songs."

Archie took a seat in a rocker and rubbed his chin. "Hows about I let you pick whatever you want? Maybe a hymn and a traditional mountain tune."

"I have to say, you don't waste no time," Drusie said, hoping to stall him. She wanted to play for Archie, but she hadn't thought he'd go in for the kill before they could sit a spell.

Archie looked at his watch. "I don't have time to waste. Time is money."

Drusie wasn't sure his philosophy was the best way to go about living, but to be agreeable, she nodded.

Gladdie handed her the banjo, and she sat back in the rocker. After thinking a moment, she selected her favorite tune, one that she knew would show off her voice. She looked back and forth at both men. Pride made Gladdie's eyes glow.

Mrs. Gordon came back out on the porch and joined them long enough to hear the songs. She clapped and smiled after the performance of the first tune and asked for another.

As she complied, Drusie tried not to linger long on Archie's face, but she could see interest and contemplation when she met his eyes. At one point when she caught Archie's glance, she almost forgot the familiar words to her song. From the intensity in his gray eyes, she could see that how well she performed was important.

When she was finished singing, everyone applauded.

Archie grinned. "Gladdie didn't exaggerate. You're very good."

"Thank you."

"Yep, Drusie does me proud every time. Sing him another song, sweetheart," Gladdie prodded.

"Another song? Don't you reckon he's right tired of hearin' me?"

"Not yet," Archie said. "I want you to show me you can perform on short notice anytime. Try 'Down in the Willow Garden.'"

So this was truly an audition! She tamped down her nervousness and concentrated on the words to the song. The old tune told about a man who killed the one he loved with a saber. Its melody sounded sweet to the ears. One had to listen closely to realize the brutality of the act described.

"Very poignant," Archie said after the last note. "How about one more?"

Drusie wasn't sure what he meant by "poignant," but she took it as a compliment and then launched into "Who's That Knocking at My Door?" After she was through, the air fell silent.

"You have quite a repertoire."

Drusie wished he wouldn't keep using such strange words, even though he smiled as he said them.

Archie stood, exuding confidence. "I think the music industry is ready for her. Lots of acts are making good with the music of home, the music we grew up with."

"Our mountain music sure is special," Mrs. Gordon agreed. "Nothin' like them city folks hear in them fancy opera houses they go to, I imagine."

"Nothing like it. And I think that's why that music sells so well. But I must say, the audience for our type of music isn't really highbrow people in New York and places like that. The people who buy our music are good, hardworking country folk," Archie explained. "The music that I record at my studio reaches a large audience, and many of them are willing to buy a record or two."

"That's all fine and good, but I don't see what any of this has to do with Drusie," Gladdie said.

"You don't?" Archie poked Gladdie. "This won't be a trip for biscuits, will it?"

"Biscuits?" Mrs. Gordon asked. "I thought you liked biscuits. Matter of fact, I made a batch up just for you."

"Oh, I like your biscuits, Aunt Penny. I just mean, I don't want to waste my time." Archie looked at Drusie. "So what do you think?"

Unwilling to appear foolish and vain, Drusie decided she'd better get Archie to spell out his intentions for business, if he had any. "Think about what?"

"Leaving this place for something better."

"Leavin'?" Gladdie let go of Drusie's hand. "I don't much like that idea."

Drusie wasn't sure what to say. She had hoped Archie would like her singing, but at that moment, she realized she hadn't thought through everything his good opinion might mean. If he wanted her to perform for a crowd, he'd want her to leave home. Suddenly she wasn't so sure. She wasn't so sure about anything. "Why, I—I don't know."

Drusie observed her surroundings. Lush foliage was everywhere, along with birds that woke her in the morning with their singing and deer that would sometimes peer at her when she was in the yard. The majesty of Grandfather Mountain never failed to inspire. She took in a breath that was a little deeper than usual, enjoying the fresh air. "There's a lot to love about this place."

"True. But there's a big world out there, and I think they're ready for you." Archie studied her. "And they'd be willing to pay money to see a pretty canary like you sing. Wouldn't you like to have a few of the finer things in life?" He cut his glance to his automobile.

Drusie shrugged. "I wouldn't mind buying Ma some things for the house, and maybe a new truck for Pa, but I don't need nothin' for myself. The good Lord provides us with all we need. But I do have a dream. I mean, Gladdie does."

"You mean, the store?" Gladdie asked.

"That's exactly what I mean," Drusie answered.

"And?" Archie let the word hang in the air.

Drusie ignored the nervous knot in her stomach. "Gladdie has his eye on a store he'd like to buy."

"Goode's Mercantile," Gladdie elaborated. "You must have passed it on your way here. It's just up the road a piece. But I don't know what that has to do with anything."

"You'll see." Drusie reached for Gladdie's hand and held it.

"Sure, I remember the store," Archie answered. "The old man's been here as long as I can recall. He and the Moore family have always tried to outdo each other. Sure you want to take over and get in the middle of all that rivalry, Gladdie?"

"Well, Mr. Goode's ready to retire now, and this may be the only chance I get to own the store. I'm sure, with the Lord's help, I can handle whatever competition anybody else in these here parts has to offer." Gladdie tightened his lips.

"That's the way I like to hear you talk." Drusie patted his shoulder and turned her face to Archie. "The Lord ain't shown Gladdie and me a way to the money yet. We want to get married, and I sure would like to help him find that money."

Archie rubbed his hands together. "Then what better way to make some bacon than singing? You've got the talent."

"I do?" Drusie could hardly believe the conversation but

decided if she really wanted to sing, she had better show some confidence. "I do!"

"You hit the nail on the head!" Archie's voice filled with cockiness. "Hows about you going with me to Raleigh? I have a recording studio, but you knew that, didn't you, doll? You can cut a record and we can sell it all over the country."

The idea, which seemed so enticing while still elusive, left her feeling unnerved now that the reality was closer. "But—nobody knows me."

"They don't know you now, but they'll know you by the time I'm done. We're going to tour, you and me. And the band, of course. We'll go all over hill country and the piedmont. Lynchburg, Roanoke, Greensboro, Charlotte, to name a few. You'll get to sing your little heart out, with professionals backing you up. Once they hear you, people everywhere will be clamoring to buy your records. I just know it."

"All that way?" She had just steeled herself for the idea of going to Raleigh. Now he was suggesting even more places. Fear struck Drusie. "Now hold on just a minute. I didn't think nothin' about goin' all over the countryside."

"How else will people get to know you?"

"I—I don't rightly know." Drusie felt dizzy. Recording? Touring? Singing in front of strangers every night? Such ideas overwhelmed her.

"You don't sound too excited."

"I'm not sure I am too excited about bein' involved in all that commotion," Drusie admitted.

Archie cast Gladdie a look. "You don't mind her going, do you? Sounds like she has plans for the money she'd make—plans that involve you." Archie punched Gladdie in the forearm. "Say, you sly dog, you didn't put her up to this, did you?"

"Why, no." Gladdie rubbed the spot where Archie's fist had made contact. "This is all her idea. She didn't say nothin' to me about it." The look Gladdie cast Drusie revealed that his feelings were hurt a mite.

"I'm sorry," Drusie apologized. "I didn't mean to keep secrets. I didn't wanna say nothin' because I didn't know for sure your cousin would like my singin'. Especially not so much that he'd make such big suggestions."

Archie chuckled. "I didn't think you were smart enough to put her up to anything."

"Hey, now!" Gladdie protested.

"I was just funning you, Gladdie. You've got one sharp dame here, and I think she'll go places if you don't hold her back. Man alive, by the time I'm finished with her, you won't just own a two-bit store out here in the middle of nowhere. You might just own a chain of stores!"

Uncertainty covered Gladdie's expression. "I just wanted her to impress you with her singin'. I had no idea things would go this far."

Archie cleared his throat. "I think it's time for me to let the two of you go it alone for a while." He rose from his seat. "Aunt Penny, have you got a glass of city juice—I mean, water?"

"Sure. And if you ask real nice, I might be able to come up with something better than that for supper. I bought two bottles of sodie pop from Mr. Goode's store, just for you. You still like sodie pop, don't ya?"

"I certainly do. Sounds good, Aunt Penny." Archie winked at Drusie. "Now you and Gladdie talk. I'll be inside if you need me."

As soon as Archie had cleared the door, Drusie took Gladdie by the hand. "I cain't believe it! I cain't believe Archie likes my singin' this much!"

"I—I'm happy and all, but I didn't think he'd make an offer to take you off to record your music. I might have known he'd only come all this way if he thought he could do some business."

"Oh, don't be so hard on your cousin. He's a busy man."

"Yeah." Gladdie didn't sound happy.

Drusie wished he were in a better mood, but she knew she had to speak up now if she had a chance of making a record. "I know it's hard, but don't you see? If I sing for this record, I might make enough money for us to get married and buy the store."

"I know. You planned this, didn't you?" His voice held no reprimand or accusation.

"I reckon I have to admit I did, after I realized he was visitin'. I thought, why not take a chance? I knew if the Lord didn't want this to happen for me, it wouldn't. But Archie hadn't been here five minutes before he asked me to sing. That's got to be a sign, doesn't it?"

"I don't know. I admit, I bragged on you mightily. Should have known better than to brag to a record producer."

"That's just it. Archie is the only person who can help us get the store. I don't want to be no big celebrity like the women in the Carter family. I just want to sing long enough for us to save up and buy the store."

"Really?"

"You know me. Archie's talk about riches don't matter to me none. Once we buy that store, all I want is to entertain my family and be Mrs. Gladdie Gordon."

"And you will be. I promise. I'm more proud of you than ever. And that you would do this for me, for us. . . I—I don't know what to say."

"Don't say nothin'. Just let me go."

"So your ma and pa don't mind?"

"Ma and Pa?" Her chest tightened. She hadn't thought they might disapprove, but they might. They never had much use for any type of show business. "I'm an adult and I can do what I want."

"Maybe in the legal sense, but not in your heart. And as long as we're not married yet, I want you to get their permission."

Drusie wanted to argue, but when Gladdie got that determined set of his jaw, there was no way he'd change his mind. They'd have to ask her parents. She could only hope they wouldn't put up too much of a fuss. If they did, Drusie saw no way for Gladdie's dream to come true.

three

Drusie wanted some time to discuss her future with Gladdie, but Archie didn't leave them on the Gordons' porch long. When he returned, he had taken off his suit coat yet still maintained his swagger and confidence. "So have you two decided to take the road to fame and fortune and let Drusie come along with me?"

"Not yet," Gladdie said. "But I have to admit, I'm warmin' up to the idea of Drusie singin' for the public. Her talent shouldn't be kept a secret forever."

"That's the spirit." Archie looked at Drusie coolly. "So when are we leaving? Tomorrow?"

"Not so fast," Gladdie said. "We have to be sure this plan is okay with Drusie's ma and pa."

"Is she that young?" Archie studied Drusie, wide-eyed.

"No," Gladdie insisted. "Have you been away from home that long? People around here still respect their parents."

"Yeah." Sadness penetrated Archie's handsome face. Drusie remembered that Archie had lost his parents young, thanks to the influenza epidemic.

"I'm sorry," Gladdie blurted, obviously remembering Archie's loss. "I didn't mean to bring up bad memories. I know you'd respect your ma and pa if they was still around."

"Yeah." Archie cleared his throat. "Your ma said I could stay here as long as I want. Might as well. But I've got to have an answer early tomorrow."

"Will do. Maybe even sooner than that." Gladdie's cheerful assurance lifted the pall in the air.

"I think I'll go get me some more of that city juice." Archie disappeared into the house.

As soon as his cousin was out of sight, Gladdie took Drusie's hand. "Are you ready to ask your pa?"

"I don't know. I hadn't given it much thought before you mentioned he might not approve. Truth be told, I reckon I hadn't given any thought to what would happen if Archie actually liked my singin'. I warn't at all sure he'd want to cut a record with me. It was a dream. . .until now."

Gladdie squeezed her hand. "And you're scared."

"A little."

"I am, too, but not about you bein' famous or travelin' with Archie. I just hate that you won't be around no more."

"Oh, Gladdie, I'll come back sooner than you can say 'boo.' And I wouldn't go with Archie, 'ceptin' he's your cousin and all."

"That's right. Your pa don't got nothin' to worry about, and neither do you. If you go with Archie, everything will be right and proper. You can trust Archie on that. I've talked to him a lot about his business, and I know he keeps his singers protected. And if anything was to happen to you, well, he'll answer to me." Gladdie puffed out his chest, and Drusie knew he meant his threat.

His bravado shored up Drusie's private concern. "All righty, then. Let's go ask Pa what he thinks."

Gladdie turned to the front door and shouted to Mrs. Gordon inside that they were leaving. Her muffled response assured them she understood.

Since their houses were within walking distance of one another, Gladdie didn't bother to fire up the Model T. Instead, they ambled along a dusty cow path that meandered along the hillside from homestead to homestead. Since they didn't speak, only an occasional rustle of leaves from a little animal or the chirping of a bird made them aware they weren't alone.

Drusie took in the stillness. All too soon, she'd be in the city, far away from her beloved mountains. A city park wouldn't have such dramatic woods as those in a hollow that dropped off to one side of the path. In the deepest, shadiest parts of the forest, she could happily get lost in God's creation.

"What are you thinkin'?" Gladdie's gentle voice broke the silence.

"Not much. Just thinkin' about the forest. And fairy tales."

He chuckled. "Fairy tales? Are you already imaginin' you're Cinderella and your dreams will all come true?"

"I was thinkin' about Little Red Ridin' Hood and the forest. I'm already Cinderella, because I've met my Prince Charmin'."

Gladdie stopped and turned so they faced one another. He took both of her hands in his. They were hot, but she didn't mind. She just wanted to look into his deep brown eyes.

"I know you're my princess," he told her. "Always have been. Just wish I had a castle instead of a little home in the mountains to offer you."

"A little home in the mountains is all I want, as long as you're there."

"I cain't wait to marry you." He gave her a gentle kiss on the lips that grew in passion, expressing his love for her. Strong arms held her closely.

Returning his embrace, she marveled at how soft his lips felt, yet so manly. Tingles went through her body, and she pulled back from his embrace. "Come on. Let's go."

"You seem mighty anxious to talk to your pa all of a sudden." His voice sounded husky.

"Anxious, yes. But not to talk to Pa." She broke away from his spell and took a fast pace toward home.

Soon they were in sight of the house Pa and his brothers had built back at the turn of the century. The log house had aged well. Drusie imagined the homestead being there long after she had passed on to glory.

She almost wished Pa wouldn't be home, but no doubt he would just be finishing up lunch.

As soon as they stepped into the kitchen, Pa eyed her from his position at the head of the table, where he sat in the only chair that had arms. "Where you been, girl?"

Drusie eyed Ma, who was stoking the fire. The tantalizing scents of vegetable stew and biscuit dough filled the kitchen. Maybe such good food would help ease Pa's reaction to their news.

Ma eyed Pa. "Don'tcha remember, Zeke? Gladdie's cousin came in today. Drusie went to his house to visit and play the banjo."

"Where's your banjo?" Pa asked.

"Still at Gladdie's house. I plan to go back and fetch it later."

"I see." Pa looked at Gladdie, his rugged face expressing warmth for his future son-in-law. "How is Archie, anyhow?"

"He's doin' better'n ever. Wearin' a fancy city-slicker suit and everything," Gladdie answered.

"I see." The older man crossed arms that were muscular from years of work. "Now if I recollect right, ain't he the one that run off to Raleigh to be in the music business?"

"Sure is," Gladdie confirmed. "Owns his own record company and everything."

Pa let out a whistle. "Well, that's mighty fine. So are you stayin' a spell, or are you back off to do some more visitin'?"

"I cain't stay too long. I have to help Pa with the animals pretty soon." Gladdie's flat tone indicated this was far from his favorite chore.

"That's right. We shouldn't tarry long." Drusie wanted to sit, but she noticed that Ma was tidying up the kitchen and decided to help. Besides, wiping down the table would help her work off some nervous energy.

Gladdie took in a breath and looked Pa in the eye. "Drusie and I have some news."

"Is that so?" Pa smiled. "You two gettin' hitched?"

Gladdie leaned back with such force that Drusie thought he might knock over his seat. "Oh, it's not that, sir. But I want to get married as soon as we can. Real bad."

Drusie quickly agreed. "And so do I."

"But Drusie has somethin' else to do first," Gladdie elaborated.

"Somethin' else to do?" Ma intervened. "What in the world would she have to do other than be a wife and maybe a mother one day, Lord willin'?"

Gladdie cleared his throat again.

"Boy, you sure are coughin' an awful lot. You don't got one of them summer colds comin' on, do ya?" Pa asked.

"No, sir."

Seeing Gladdie so uncharacteristically nervous, Drusie decided to intervene. "Oh, Pa, we've got the most wonderful news. Archie wants me to go to Raleigh and make a record!"

Pa's eyebrows shot up. "A record?"

Ma almost dropped her spoon. "Well, that's somethin'!"

Drusie nodded. "Isn't it excitin'?"

Gladdie seemed to get caught up in the moment. A torrent of words rushed from him. "Archie heard Drusie play and sing today, and he wants to take her to Raleigh so she can cut a record. After that, they'll tour with a band and be known all over the country. Maybe even all over the world. Everyone will know Drusie's name and buy her records and pay money to see her play."

Ma gasped. "Imagine! Strangers payin' Drusie money for what we get to hear around these parts for free."

"Well, if that don't beat all." Pa tugged on his graying beard.

"Archie mentioned that I might make enough money to buy fine things, so he must be thinkin' my singin' is worth right much money," Drusie said. "But I don't want to live like one of them silent film stars. What I really want is for Gladdie to buy Mr. Goode's store. All I want to do is sell a few records, make enough money to help Gladdie buy the store, and then come back here and live."

Her parents knew about Gladdie's dream, so Drusie's announcement about the store was no revelation. Her new plans for a brief musical career were another matter. She could see by the quizzical looks on their faces that they were trying to sort out what her news meant for the family.

Ma recovered first. "You gotta leave home?"

"I don't want to leave," Drusie assured her. "I need to. I have to go with Archie to Raleigh. But I won't need to stay long. Hardly no time at all."

Pa remained unmoved. "Now hold on. He wants to take her to Raleigh?"

"He sure does," Gladdie confirmed.

Pa looked at Drusie. "What do you think of all this?"

Drusie folded the damp cloth. "I want to go with Archie Gordon to Raleigh."

"Now wait a minute. I don't think it's wise for you to go alone with a man to Raleigh—or anywhere else—when the two of you ain't married. Remember, the Bible says to avoid all appearance of evil." Pa studied Gladdie. "Cain't Drusie stay here at home where she belongs? The mountains are good enough for us. They should be good enough for her. I don't think she should go."

Ma spoke as she tended the fire. "But Zeke, I don't see why she cain't give it a try. Just because you didn't have a chance like this don't mean we should keep our daughter from tryin', does it? Besides, I don't know of no other way Gladdie can buy the store. Do you?"

Pa set his elbows on the table. "I won't argue that. And

Gladdie, you know I think you're a mighty fine feller, and I don't want to stand in the way of you and Drusie havin' a good life. And ownin' that store would mean a good life for the two of you. I'm just saying it don't look right for a young lady to go travelin' on the road with a man."

"It will only be until we get to Raleigh," Drusie said. "If we leave well before sunup, we can get there without havin' to stop on the road for the night."

"Archie has a lot of female singers he manages. I know he makes arrangements for them to stay places that are safe for women," Gladdie said. "Then they'll be travelin' with the band."

"A bunch of men?" Pa scoffed. "I think she'd be much safer here with us. Don't you, Gladdie?"

Gladdie didn't answer right away, a sure sign he wanted to weigh his words. "I understand how you feel, but she'll be safe. I know there will be female performers other than Drusie goin' along. Like I said, sir, Archie has lots of girl singers he manages. He usually takes more than one band on tour at a time."

"He does, does he?" Suspicion hung in Pa's voice.

"It's all professional."

"Oh, Zeke," Ma interrupted. "If you would trust Gladdie to marry our Drusie, cain't you trust him to give advice on Drusie's future?"

He crossed his arms, but his cocked head showed he was still listening. "Well, you have a point, wife."

"Of course I have a point. Now this sounds like a good opportunity for Drusie. You know she cain't do nothin' around these parts but be a schoolteacher, and it don't look like Miss Hawthorne plans to marry anytime soon and give up her job. And besides," Ma continued, "you know I always wished I coulda made a dollar or two playin' music."

Drusie's mouth dropped open. "You did? Ma, I never knew."

"Child, you look like you're about to swallow a fly." Ma swatted her hand in Drusie's direction. "Now my little attempts at music warn't nothin'."

"Nothin'?" Pa protested. "Why, you was the best girl singer in the holler back in our day."

Ma looked over the fire. "That was a long time ago, Zeke."

"Oh, Ma, I've heard you sing. You can outdo me any day of the week."

"So what kept you from goin' on about makin' your dream come true, Mrs. Fields?" Gladdie wanted to know.

"You're about to marry one of the reasons," she responded. "I wanted to have children. And I wouldn't trade a one of my girls for all the money or fame in the world."

"Oh, Ma!" Drusie cried.

"Now, now, don't you say nothin'. I wanted to marry your pa more than anything, and I gave up my dream to do it. Not that it really was much of a dream. Back then, I didn't have no chance to make good in the city, and even if I had, I'm not sure I could have left home. I would have been too unhappy. And your pa wanted to work in the loggin' business, just like his pa before him. He didn't have no idea to own a store. And back then, makin' records warn't nothin' as easy as it is now, and show folk traveled by train." She smiled at Gladdie. "I don't see no reason why Drusie should give up her chance, especially to make such a big dream like yours come true, too, Gladdie. I think you'd make a fine storekeeper. You already make a fine clerk." She looked at her husband. "Ain't that right, Zeke?"

"Cain't deny it."

Ma looked at Drusie without flinching. "Gladdie seems to think it's a mighty fine thing for you to work with Archie, and if that's what he thinks, and since he's your intended, I think you ought to obey him. Preacher Lawson says we ought to obey our husbands. Remember when he said that?"

"I remember, Ma." Drusie felt girded by such encouragement. Surely God had used her mother to speak to her. It wasn't the first time. "What do you say, Pa?"

Pa rubbed his bearded chin. "Well, when you put it like that, I reckon I oughtta give you my blessing."

"Thank you, Pa!" Drusie embraced him.

"Thank you, Mr. Fields!" Gladdie rose from his seat and took Drusie by the hand. "Come on and let's tell Archie. We've got a lot to talk about."

"Hold your horses," Pa said. "There's somethin' else. A condition I have for you. And if you two don't go along with what I say, I cain't allow Drusie to go."

four

Watching Pa as he sat still in his kitchen chair, Drusie felt as though she were a rock by the side of the creek, water rushing at her, unable to move. So Pa had a condition as to whether or not she could go to Raleigh and cut a record of the music of home. Now that it looked like Pa was about to throw a monkey wrench into her new plans, she couldn't help but feel disappointed.

What could the condition be? She tried to guess. Could he want Gladdie to marry her before she left? She suppressed a smile. Such a thought could make sense. After all, she'd never dream of taking her music to the world outside her mountain community except that Gladdie wanted to buy the store and she wanted to make enough money so that would be possible. Maybe Pa wanted to make sure Gladdie was tied to her right good before she made all that effort for him. Drusie trusted Gladdie, and if Pa said they had to get hitched before he would agree to let her go to Raleigh, Drusie wouldn't mind that at all.

Her heart reminded her of its existence by beating fast in her chest. She took in a breath. "What's the condition, Pa?"

He eyed Gladdie, then Drusie. "I want you to take Clara with you."

"Clara?" Drusie blurted. Her mind switched gears to cope with such an unexpected turn of events. Clara, going with them to Raleigh? To cut the record with her? Sure, Clara sang like a bird, but Drusie never thought about her sister even wanting to go.

"Yep." Pa nodded. "She sings real good. You two sound even better together than either one of you sounds by yourself. And havin' a sister along means you can look out for each other—just in case you find yourself in a situation you warn't meanin' to."

Gladdie interrupted with a protest. "But Mr. Fields, I won't let nothin' happen to Drusie. She means too much to me."

"You goin' along?"

"Uh, no, sir," Gladdie admitted, glancing at his feet and back to Mr. Fields. "I have to stay here and help my family."

"Well then," Pa said, "to my way of thinkin', you cain't help Drusie much if you're here and she's all the way in Raleigh. Now I don't mean no disrespect, son. I know you'd never set your mind to lettin' somethin' happen to her, but the outside world can be a mighty mean place where bad things can happen. Terrible bad things. She needs protection. Now you say that your cousin has women travelin' with the band, but them women just ain't gonna look after Drusie the way her own sister would."

"I understand, sir." Gladdie's voice registered defeat.

"Well then, her sister needs to go, to my way of thinking, and there ain't nothin' you or Archie or anyone else can say to change my mind on that. So either both sisters go, or nobody goes. That's my final word." The way Pa looked right into Gladdie's brown eyes without flinching told Drusie that he meant what he said.

Anxiety clutched Drusie in her gut. What if Clara didn't want to go? Even more likely, what if Archie didn't want Clara to go along? Then Drusie's chances of helping Gladdie buy the store would be ruined. Mr. Goode would sell it to someone else, and they'd never have another chance. She didn't like debating with Pa, but this time she felt she had to kick up a fuss. She reached for an argument. "So you're gonna send

Clara along and endanger her, too?"

"I believe in the old sayin' that there's safety in numbers. And Clara would look after you. And you'll look after her." He wagged his forefinger at her, shaking it on each word for emphasis.

She tried again. "I know that, Pa. I'll be so busy lookin' after her that I won't have time to sing."

When Drusie cut her glance to Gladdie, she noticed he rubbed his fingertips together. She figured he was thinking his way out of the situation, too. "Mr. Fields, I worry that if we insist, it might ruin Drusie's chances," Gladdie said. "Archie didn't agree to let another person come along. Travelin' is expensive, and she'd be another mouth to feed."

"And another mouth to sing, too," Pa pointed out.

"So do you think Clara would want to make a record?" Gladdie wondered aloud. "It's one thing to sing at church, but it's a horse of another color to sing on a record for the whole world."

"True. Why don't we ask her and find out?" Pa didn't wait for an answer before he hollered out Clara's name.

Ma stopped tending the pot of stew long enough to answer. "I sent her to fetch some water from the well. She's been gone long enough that she oughtta be back anytime now."

Pa rose from his seat and peered out the back door. "She's comin' on up here now."

"Maybe I should go help her," Gladdie said.

"Naw," Pa said. "She's got to learn to handle that bucket herself."

Silence fell upon them as they waited for Clara to struggle with getting the water to the house in a heavy wooden bucket. Drusie never minded when it was her turn to fetch water. She enjoyed walking outdoors, down the narrow path to the well. The time alone gave her a few minutes to think and to enjoy God's creation. Her least favorite part of the journey was carrying the burdensome bucket filled to the brim. Not splashing half the supply out onto the ground was the trick to not making a second trip to the well. After many tries, Drusie became skilled at carrying water without spilling a drop, something she took pride in. Clara never did become quite so adept, and hence she complained whenever it was her turn to do the fetching. But by walking slowly, she managed to keep most of the water in the bucket.

Nervous, Drusie looked at the fire and contemplated stoking it while they waited.

"Drusie," Gladdie asked, "would you mind fixin' me a glass of water?"

"Sure." She hurried to comply, grateful for the simple task. By the time she was done, Clara had entered the kitchen with fresh water.

"Hey, Gladdie." She set down the water and glanced from Gladdie, to Drusie, to Ma, and then to Pa. "What's the matter? Y'all look like there's bad news brewin'. There ain't nothin' wrong, is there?" She paled.

"No, Clara. Nothin's wrong," Pa assured. "Sit on down." He nodded to an empty chair.

She obeyed. "What is it, Pa?"

"Didn't Drusie tell you that she and Gladdie would be seein' his cousin Archie today? The one that run off to Raleigh and has his own recordin' studio now?"

"I remember Archie. Skinny and hardly old enough to think for himself when he left here. So he made good?"

"Real good." Gladdie's voice was filled with pride.

"That's nice." Clara's posture relaxed. Obviously, she thought Archie's visit had nothing to do with her.

Pa leaned forward. "How would you like to sing with Drusie, in front of people, for pay?"

"For pay?" Clara laughed so hard she snorted. "Who'd pay us to sing?"

"Lots of people, accordin' to Gladdie's cousin Archie."

Clara turned serious. "What? You mean Archie wants me to sing? He has the power to make such a big decision on his own?" She gasped, her voice showing a mixture of excitement and uncertainty.

"He sure does. He owns the studio and everything," Pa said.

"True, but everything ain't exactly set," Gladdie said. "At least, not yet. You've gotten to be part of the deal if Archie plans to take Drusie."

Clara crossed her arms like a petulant child. "Care to explain?"

Drusie elaborated on the day's events. As she did, Clara went from lazing back in her chair, displaying the interest of a schoolchild at the end of a two-hour sermon, to leaning forward, mouth open and eyes wide.

"That's swell!" Clara said after Drusie concluded. "So Archie wants you to be a big-time singer, and with our humble mountain music at that." She shook her head. "Who'd've thought such a thing?"

"I know it's mighty amazin'," Drusie said. "So don't ya wanna go?"

"I don't rightly think I do."

Drusie's jaw slackened with disappointment. "But you got to, Clara! You just got to! If you don't, me and Gladdie will never get to buy the store."

"I know all about your dreams, and I'd like to help, but I cain't." She turned up her nose ever so slightly. "If I'm second fiddle, I don't want no part of this record business. I can stay here and be second fiddle to everybody else."

"I'll be happy for you to take the lead on some of the songs, Clara." Drusie set her hand on her sister's knee and held her gaze to show Clara her sincerity. "I'd welcome it. I don't need to sing so much that I don't have a voice left."

"Aw, come on, Clara," Gladdie prodded. "You and Drusie will have fun. You'll meet lots of people and have some cash."

"Cash money?" Clara shifted so that Drusie's hand fell from her knee.

Drusie leaned against the back of her chair. With Clara's renewed attentiveness, hope sparked.

"How much money?" Clara wanted to know.

Guilt marred Drusie's happiness. Remembering biblical admonitions about the love of money, she felt reluctant to use its lure as an argument to sway her sister, but desperation drove her. "Archie said somethin' to me about buyin' fine things."

"Fine things?" Clara's mouth hung open. "You mean, we can make that much money?"

Drusie shrugged. "I reckon."

Clara's eyes became dreamy. "I always have wanted to wear pretty clothes."

"Pretty clothes?" Ma objected. "Don't you think you got pretty clothes now?"

Clara turned her mouth into a sheepish line. "Yes, ma'am. You make me pretty dresses all the time. It's just that I can just imagine wearin' store-bought clothes every day."

"I don't suppose you can be blamed," Ma admitted. "You're young, and you can enjoy the finer things in life that we never had." She shook her head. "Imagine!"

"Clara won't have to imagine long, if what Archie says is true," Gladdie observed.

Clara rose from her seat and nodded once in a way that showed her mind was made up. "Okay. I'll go."

"Now money isn't everything," Pa cautioned. "If riches is what you want, maybe it's not such a good idea for you to go after all."

"Why else would I want to go, Pa?" As soon as the question left Clara's mouth, she twisted her lips and looked at her sister. "I know. You want me to keep Drusie out of trouble."

"That won't be hard. I don't plan on gettin' into trouble," Drusie assured her.

Clara cocked her head and pointed at her sister. "You better not. If I'm ever gonna be famous, I won't have time to look after you."

Pa's laughter filled the kitchen. "Then it's settled."

"Not quite yet, Mr. Fields." Gladdie wore a worried look that Drusie didn't like. "Like I said, my cousin Archie ain't agreed to your plan for two singin' sisters."

"I know it, Gladdie, but Clara deserves to make good in the city, just as Drusie does," Pa persisted. "So you tell your cousin if he wants Drusie, he has to take Clara, too."

"I'll tell him that, sir." Although he kept from frowning, disappointment etched Gladdie's voice.

Drusie kept her face unreadable. Pa never said it aloud, but he favored Clara. True, she was open about her emotions, filling the room with optimism whenever she entered and displaying cuteness even when disagreeable. Drusie was the serious, studious one—harder for people to get to know. Sometimes she wished she was more like her little sister. But God had fashioned them both for His reasons. Drusie had learned to live with their differences long ago.

Given their past history, she wasn't surprised that Pa had managed to turn her opportunity into one that would benefit her sister. Still, it would be nice to have Clara along. "Gladdie's right. Besides, Archie cain't decide nothin' without hearin' Clara sing." She motioned to her sister. "Come on. Pick up your fiddle and let's go to Gladdie's house. Archie's there now. You can audition, and he can tell us what he thinks."

"Is that okay with you, Pa?" Clara asked.

He nodded. "Makes sense to me."

Clara clapped, reminding Drusie of a little girl. "Let me put on my Sunday dress and clean up a little. It won't take me long, I promise." Without further ado, she exited.

Drusie could see from her level of intensity that she'd be dressed faster than a cow could swing her tail to shoo a fly.

Moments later, Clara emerged wearing a Sunday dress with a polka-dotted pattern that fit her form well, but not too tightly.

"You look nice," Ma said.

Clara patted her shiny light brown curls. "I hope so."

Without pause, Gladdie, Drusie, and Clara bid Ma and Pa good-bye and were on their way around the hill and past the hollow to the Gordons'. The walk back was more of a stride, and nothing that could be called romantic. This was a business trip.

"So," Clara asked, "do you think Archie will like me?"

"I don't see why not," Drusie assured her. "You were a pretty little girl when he left, and you're even prettier now." She lowered her voice, even though they were well out of earshot from the house. "I didn't want to say this in front of Pa, but I imagine Archie will start describin' you in terms of food as soon as he sets eyes on you."

Clara scrunched her eyebrows. "Food?"

"Things like 'dish' and 'tomato' is what he likes to say. I don't understand what he's talkin' about half the time, but he seems to think he's bein' nice. City ways—you know."

"I'll try to catch on," Clara said with a grin. "I just hope he thinks I'm pretty."

"You have to be more than pretty," Gladdie said, though not in an unkind tone. "You have to sing well enough for him to decide he wants to make a record with you. Archie is a businessman, and they don't like to lose money."

"I can imagine he don't."

"What do you think you'll sing?" Drusie asked.

"I don't rightly know." She paused to think. " 'Cindy' and 'Mole in the Ground' maybe."

"I can sing along with you on one so he can see how we do together," Drusie suggested. "Let's sing a hymn, too. He likes that."

"Okay."

They approached the Gordons' house, where Archie waited on the porch. Instead of rocking in a chair, he stood with one hand on his hip, looking at the horizon.

Clara stopped and took in a breath.

Drusie followed suit. "What's the matter?"

"N—nothin'. Uh, is that Archie?"

"Sure is," Gladdie affirmed.

Clara kept staring. "He's all growed up!"

Something in Clara's tone and sudden change in posture made Drusie nervous. If she decided to get a crush on Archie before she even spoke to him, Pa would figure that out right quick, and their trip would be doomed. "Now he's a big record producer, and we're just one of his acts—we hope. So don't go gettin' any ideas," Drusie hissed at her sister. "Come on." Drusie tugged on her arm, prodding her to resume walking.

Clara pouted but kept her voice low. "I ain't got no ideas. You're always thinkin' somethin' like that."

Drusie remembered how Clara liked to flirt with all the eligible bachelors but decided not to make further mention of that fact. Instead, she sent a silent prayer that the audition would go well. As long as Clara could concentrate on her singing and not too much on the brash redheaded man standing on the porch, surely everything would be just fine.

She hoped.

five

Gladdie watched his cousin Archie stare at Drusie and Clara as they approached. Jealousy sparked through him until he looked more closely and saw that Archie wasn't studying Drusie, but Clara. He cut his glance to Drusie's sister and noticed she couldn't take her gaze from him, either. The idea made him uneasy. Archie was too much of a gentleman—and a businessman—to be forward with any of his singers. Still, Archie was a man who had an eye for the ladies, and Gladdie could feel tension emanating from him that hadn't been present until the moment the women came into view.

Lord, Thy will be done.

Gladdie wanted to elaborate on his prayer, but no words entered his mind. Everything had happened so quickly. What had started as a visit from Archie had turned into a business deal. Gladdie freely admitted that he had wanted Drusie to impress his cousin with her singing. He thought earning compliments from someone in the music business would make Drusie happy. That was all he wanted. All he ever wanted. Even his idea to buy the store was motivated by a desire to make a better life for them both.

As soon as Drusie showed up with her banjo, Gladdie realized from Archie's eagerness to hear her perform that auditioning Gladdie's fiancée was the real reason for the visit, not a family reunion. Archie was a businessman through and through, all right.

Conflicting feelings wouldn't leave Gladdie alone. He wanted to buy the store, and with Mr. Goode's retirement happening ahead of schedule, Gladdie could be required to come up with the money quickly. Too quickly. Drusie's success in the music business was the only way he could see that happening. But he didn't want to depend on his future wife to earn the money. To him, sending her out into the cold world didn't seem fair, no matter how much she wanted to go.

Gladdie left his own thoughts long enough to see that Archie gazed at Clara, who looked at him in return. He expected Archie to start talking about food, but for once, he seemed speechless. Gladdie cleared his throat. "Archie, do you recollect Clara Fields?"

Recognition flickered in his eyes. "I do! You're Drusie's little sister, all grown up?"

Clara looked him straight in the eyes before she decided to study the hem of her skirt in a demure manner. "That's me."

"You sure have grown up." Archie's voice had lost its usual brashness.

Drusie smiled. "That's just what she said about you."

Clara poked Drusie in the ribs. "Drusie!"

"There ain't nothin' wrong with what you said. It's just a fact."

Archie didn't take his gaze from Clara's face. "Yeah. It's a fact."

Gladdie wondered at the scene. Instead of his usual slang, Archie spoke in terms regular people could understand. For a moment, it seemed as though the old Archie he knew and liked had returned.

"It's—uh, sure nice to see you," Archie said.

"Why don't you sit down?" Gladdie suggested. "I have a reason for bringin' Clara to see you."

Gladdie's ma chose that moment to interrupt. "I thought I heard voices out here. Hello, Clara. My, you look pretty in your Sunday best. I always say the Fields girls are the prettiest around." She winked at Drusie, which made Gladdie feel proud and happy that his mother liked her.

"Today's special. Our Archie is home." Mrs. Gordon took Archie's chin in her hand and wiggled his clean-shaven skin with the affection of an aunt.

Gladdie remembered his responsibilities. "Could you let Pa know I'll be there to help in a few minutes?"

Ma cackled. "He's in a right good mood today. He said you can have the afternoon off this once."

"Well, hows about that?" Gladdie smiled. Realizing he didn't need to rush off to do chores left him feeling at ease.

"Supper will be ready shortly." Ma disappeared into the house.

"I would have offered to help, but she went in too fast," Clara said.

Gladdie tried not to smile. Enthusiasm for housework wasn't going to get Clara a husband; her pretty face would. "Ma can take care of supper. Besides, we need you out here."

"You do? Let's hear what's on your mind." Archie took a seat in a rocker.

Gladdie took in a breath before letting the words spill. "Mr. Fields said Drusie cain't go without Clara. He wants them to look out for each other."

Archie crossed his arms. "I see. He doesn't trust me, eh? Seems he'd know by now that a Gordon can be trusted."

"I know," Gladdie agreed.

"Please try not to let your feelin's get hurt," Drusie said. "Pa don't mean no harm. He just don't want nothin' to happen to any of us girls, that's all."

"I can respect that." Archie tapped his lips with his forefinger. "There's only one problem. I can't afford to take you both."

Gladdie's emotions roiled at Archie's admission. He didn't want Drusie to leave home, yet she was so excited by the prospect of helping him make a better future for them both that he hated to see the opportunity slip away with such ease. But what could he do? "I reckon that's it, then."

"Wait," Drusie objected. "Clara's a great singer. She can sing with me. We sing together all the time, and most people seem to think she and I sound better together than apart."

"They do?" Archie's voice brightened, and he leaned forward in his seat.

"They do." For the first time since before they left the Fieldses' house, Gladdie's voice held a hint of optimism.

"Won't you give her a chance to sing for you before you make up your mind, Archie? Please?" Drusie begged.

"You got time, Clara?" Archie inquired.

"I sure do."

"Sure she does. She brought her fiddle." Drusie nodded to her sister. "Didn't you, Clara?"

"I sure enough did."

Archie rocked back. "Well, I don't have anything to lose by sitting here, enjoying the mountain air and the smell of biscuits baking, listening to the two of you harmonize. Why don't you sing me a couple of tunes? Clara, you sing a number by yourself, and then sing something for me with Drusie."

Without pause, the sisters played the tunes they had talked about earlier. Gladdie observed Archie's expression as they sang. His face went from unreadable to pleased.

After three choruses, they strummed the last note, and Archie clapped. "You're swell!"

"We are?" Drusie blurted.

"Don't sound so surprised. A star has to be confident," Archie reprimanded in a playful tone. He looked at the women and sighed, shaking his head. "I must say, you live up to your promise. I sure wish I could take you both."

Gladdie wasn't one to chastise others, but he felt a challenge was in order. "But Archie, you said you have plenty of money."

"Sure, I got plenty of salad. But it costs a lot to run a show, and I got to stay to a certain budget." He shook his head again, and he looked at Clara with—what? Longing?

Clara piped up. "I'll sing for free."

"Free?" Archie quipped. "That's a price made in heaven, but I can't let you do that."

"But you think we'll be successful, right?"

"Sure. I wouldn't cut a record with you otherwise. Even if you are the prettiest doll I've seen in a long time."

Clara averted her eyes coyly but got right back to business. "If we're that good, maybe Drusie will share her profits with me." She eyed her sister. "Would you do that, Drusie? There should be plenty of money to go around if we're as good as Archie says we are."

Drusie paused only for a moment. "You're right. It makes more sense for both of us to go and split the profits than for neither of us to go at all."

Archie cast Drusie a doubtful look. "Are you sure, Drusie? You're makin' a sacrifice not everybody would make."

"She's my sister. It ain't no sacrifice. You know she's doin' me a favor by goin' since Pa won't have it any other way."

"Okay then. Maybe I can see my way clear to give you a better percentage of the profits, then. Never let it be said I took advantage of you or anybody else."

Clara beamed. "So it's settled."

"Congratulations, Miss Clara Fields. You have just joined Mountain Music Records."

Clara shook his hand and held his gaze. "Why, thanks, Archie. This is the best thing that's ever happened to me."

"Yeah." His voice was soft.

Gladdie decided to break the spell. "Clara, I'm happy for you."

"Me, too!" Drusie embraced her sister.

"Now we just need a name for our twosome." Archie's

businesslike tone had returned. "Got any suggestions?"

"I don't know," Gladdie said. "You're the professional."

"How about the Gospel Girls?" Clara suggested.

"But you'll be singing traditional mountain music, not just hymns," Archie pointed out.

The group bantered around several names.

"I know!" Archie snapped his fingers. "How about the North Carolina Mountain Girls?"

"Ain't that a mite long? Can anybody remember all that?" Gladdie wondered. "Might not be bad if we shorten it to the NC Mountain Girls."

Archie gazed at the sky. "The NC Mountain Girls." He paused. "Hmm. Not bad. Okay, let's go with that, then."

"Good. Now we can relax," Clara said.

"Relax?" Archie laughed. "You're just getting started. You've got to sign the contract. He reached into an inner pocket in his suit coat and handed Drusie some papers.

She read the contract as Gladdie and Clara peered over her shoulders. "Looks like a bunch of legal gibberish. I want Pa to sign for me."

"Them papers is nothin' but Greek to me," Clara said. "I want Pa to sign for me, too."

Drusie pointed to blank lines. "What's this for?"

Archie glanced at the lines. "Oh, those. That's to fill in the dates the contract is good for. I'll fill that in and let your pa initial it."

"How come it's a set time like that?" Gladdie asked.

"For everybody's protection. If things don't work out, it's easier to let the contract expire than to have to break a binding legal agreement," Archie said.

"Makes sense," Gladdie said.

"Fine with me." Drusie handed the papers back to Archie.

He returned the papers to his pocket. "I'll go see your father, and as soon as he signs, we'll begin. I have a tour in mind you can join. It starts a few days after I'm—*we're* scheduled to get back to Raleigh."

Drusie swallowed. "So soon?"

"The sooner the better," Archie answered. "Pack your bags. We're heading out tomorrow."

❧

After supper, Gladdie made a point of taking Drusie for a walk in the forest. They strolled along the narrow path they had covered together so many times before, stopping at familiar landmarks they could barely see as twilight fell.

Drusie paused at an ancient oak. Finding a heart with the couple's initials Gladdie had carved when they were in high school, she outlined the indentations with her finger. "Our own special tree. We still have the only initials carved on it."

"Remember the day I did that?"

"I sure do. It was May Day, and I was partners with Ben for the maypole dance."

"I never did like Ben much."

The sound of Drusie's laughter jingled prettily. "Mrs. Thomas set us together because he was so short and so am I. You know he always had eyes for Bobbie Sue."

"All I remember is I could hardly think about the dance, I was studyin' you so much and thinkin' about how I'd spent most of the mornin' carvin' out our initials. I didn't pay poor Hilda no mind."

"Don't worry. She was too busy flirtin' with Tab."

"Was she? I didn't notice." Gladdie placed his hands on hers and followed the motion of outlining the heart around the initials. Her soft hand felt so small and vulnerable under his. He wanted to protect her forever. How could he, when she was off to see the world without him?

Drusie didn't move her hand. "This here carvin' was quite a

surprise. I didn't even know you had a hankerin' for me. Even though I know I sure had it bad for you." She stopped moving her hand long enough to give him a sly grin. "What would you have done if I'd said I didn't love you back?"

"Oh, I reckon I would have found some other girl with the initials D.F."

"Is that what you think?" A playful slap on the arm emphasized her point. "Who's to say I wouldn't have found somebody else with your initials?"

"He wouldn't have kissed you like this." Turning serious, Gladdie took her in his arms and caressed his lips against hers. He held her for all he was worth, letting the kiss linger so Drusie wouldn't forget his love for her. Judging from the way she relaxed in his arms and pressed her lips more urgently against his, he knew she would always remember him. "We'll marry as soon as you get back from your tour," he murmured between kisses.

"Do you mean that?" She peered into his eyes.

He held her more closely. "Yes. I ain't never meant nothin' more. I love you, Drusie. You understand me?" He broke off the kiss long enough to take a little box out of his trousers pocket. "I've got something here for you. I've been savin' money for it all along."

"Gladdie! I don't want you to spend your money on me!"

He shrugged. "Who else am I gonna spend it on?"

She looked into the little box. A heart-shaped pendant with the inscription I Love You glimmered against red satin. The pendant was set on a chain so thin it looked almost transparent. She gasped. "It's beautiful! Oh, I'll wear it always!"

"You better! Here, let me put it on you."

Drusie turned around and let him fasten the hook. The pendant hung daintily around her neck. "I love it! I'll sleep in it and everything!"

"You don't have to do that, as long as you don't forget how much I love you."

"I never will." She punctuated her promise with a sweet, tender kiss.

Gladdie would have kissed her back had they not been interrupted by someone clearing his throat. He turned to see Archie.

"So there you are. Sorry. I hate to break up the party, but your pa wants to see you, Gladdie. Right away."

six

Gladdie wondered what Pa could want. Why had he sent Archie into the woods to find him? An ominous feeling visited Gladdie, but he tried to keep his voice light. "Sure, Archie." He took Drusie's hand. "Come on."

Archie shook his head. "He said he wants to see you alone. Sorry, Drusie. Gladdie, would you like me to walk her back to her house?"

"Sure." Gladdie swallowed. What could Pa want that meant he had to leave Drusie behind? He didn't like it. Not one bit.

"I hope everything's all right." Drusie's sentiment echoed his concern.

"It will be. Pray!" Gladdie blurted.

"I always do."

"At this rate, I'll even pray," Archie added. "Let's go, Drusie."

Gladdie approached his house with a sense of anxiety but kept putting one foot in front of the other until he heard Pa calling from the back. "There you are, Gladdie. Stay right there."

"Yes, sir."

Pa hollered out to the others that Gladdie had been found and to leave them be on the porch. Too fidgety to sit, Gladdie remained standing.

Soon his father appeared, looking fit and trim as always, his fine physique unable to be hidden by work clothes. Gladdie imagined he would look much like his pa if God allowed him to reach the age of forty-eight. So many years seemed a long way off.

"Sit down, son." Pa took a seat, and the tone of his voice

demanded that Gladdie obey him.

"Yes, sir." Gladdie sat. "You wanted to see me?"

"'Course I did. If I didn't, I wouldn't've called for ya." His eyes narrowed. "Now what's this I hear about you lettin' a woman earn your way?"

Hesitating, Gladdie didn't know what to say. The idea that Pa would object to their plans had never occurred to him. "Uh, is that what Ma told you?"

"No, but she did tell me you're plannin' to let Drusie go to Raleigh and sing to make money so you can buy the store. Is that right?"

"Yes, sir." Gladdie's stomach felt as though it was caught in a timber hitch knot.

Pa shook his head. "I'd've never believed such a thing if you hadn't've told me so yourself. That just won't do. Gordon men fend for themselves, and our womenfolk live on what we provide. If Drusie thinks she needs to live like a queen, she can make her own way, but you are not to take charity."

"Charity? I don't think of Drusie's singin' as charity. She's gonna be my wife." Seeing the hard look on Pa's face demoralized Gladdie. His pa had always been a stubborn soul, unwilling to accept help from anyone. Gladdie shouldn't have been surprised by his reaction, although he felt taken aback all the same. Gladdie reached for another argument. "I didn't ask her to go. She wants to go. Singin' in a band is her dream. Well, at least it is now that Archie's taken a mind to lettin' her and her sister form the NC Mountain Girls."

"So it was her idea to carry you. They even got a name for theirselves, huh?"

"Yes, sir." Gladdie hoped since the plans were already so far along that Pa wouldn't object further.

Gladdie's hopes evaporated when Pa shook his head again. "I wish them two girls the best, but all the same, I won't have people sayin' my boy had to take money from his intended like that."

He didn't want to argue with his father, but he saw no other way. "But Pa, how else am I gonna get to buy the store?"

"I've thought of that. I know you've had your eye to bein' a merchant for a long time now. Mr. Goode has been kind to you, even to the point of lettin' you have the day off so you could visit with Archie. Bein' exposed to the store like that, I can see why you got such an idea. And I think you'd be good at storekeepin', too. You got a head for figures, and people seem to like you right good."

Gladdie hadn't realized Pa had been paying so much attention to his hopes and dreams. The unaccustomed compliments from his pa, usually a taciturn man, pleased him. He took a moment to relish such golden words. "Thank you, Pa."

"Since you seem to have the ambition to make your dream come true, I think you have the determination not to waste money. So I have a plan." Pa leaned closer and lowered his voice. "Me and your ma, we got a few dollars saved up. I'll loan you the money. But you have to pay it back. With interest."

Gratitude, surprise, and excitement flooded Gladdie. "You— you'd do that for me?" He didn't recall Pa helping out his older brothers and sisters in such a manner.

"You're my son. Mebbe I'm gettin' soft in my old age. But you're my youngest, and time on this here earth is gettin' shorter and shorter for me with each passin' day. Experience has showed me that sometimes a man has to help his son out. But that don't mean all this is free. Like I said, you got to pay all the money back. If you don't, then the store's mine." Pa stood and extended his hand for a shake. "Deal?"

"Deal." Gladdie grasped his father's hand. "Thank you, Pa. I never would have thought you'd have enough money to help me out."

Mock insult covered Pa's face. "Why? Because we don't spend no more than I make? We even manage to put away a few dollars every week. I'll bet a lot of them folks in Raleigh owe money to every merchant in town. They live high on the hog. We hill folk live simple and save up money for a rainy day."

"Maybe so." Gladdie grinned. "I'm gonna follow your advice, Pa, and save up my money, too. After I pay you back."

"You do that."

"Can I go tell Drusie now?" Gladdie paused and took in a breath. "You know what? This means Drusie don't have to leave after all! She can stay here, and we can get married right away!" He had to use all his restraint to keep from whooping and hollering.

Pa smiled. "You go right ahead. But don't stay too long at her house. You've got chores to do tomorrow mornin', and then we've got to go see Mr. Goode and make our offer."

They would be making Mr. Goode an offer! The idea made him dizzy with anticipation. Without delay, Gladdie took off for Drusie's. On the way, he met Archie.

"You're making tracks!" Archie observed. "What's your hurry?"

"I'll tell you as soon as I tell Drusie." Gladdie didn't stop. If he did, Archie was sure to pry the news out of him and try to talk him into letting Drusie go to Raleigh. "I'll tell you later."

Once he reached the house, Gladdie didn't knock on the Fieldses' front door but went in and hollered a greeting.

"Gladdie?" Drusie entered the parlor. "Whatcha doin' here? I warn't expectin' to see you again until mornin'." She grinned. "But I'm sure glad you're here. We hardly had time for a proper good-bye."

Gladdie rushed to her and took her hands in his. "We don't need no time for a proper good-bye."

"What do you mean?"

"We can get married right away!"

Drusie gasped, and Gladdie noticed that the moonlight streaming through the window caught her wide eyes. "Right away? Is that what you want?"

"Sure do."

She wrapped her arms around him. Setting her cool cheek against his, she spoke gently into his ear. "We can marry before I leave. Maybe Archie will stay another day or two and consent to be your best man. Clara will be my maid of honor." She broke the embrace and called her sister.

Clara responded by bounding in without pause. "I heard! Oh, this is keen, Drusie!"

"You eavesdropper, you!" With no accusation in her voice, Drusie hugged her sister.

"Wait," Gladdie said.

"Wait?" Drusie pushed away from her sister and looked at Gladdie as though he'd just suggested that Christmas was canceled. "I don't got no time to wait. I've got loads to do."

"You don't understand. Archie won't want to be my best man after what I have to say." Gladdie set Drusie down on the sofa, with Clara observing from a nearby chair. He told Drusie what had just transpired with his pa, omitting the prideful opinions he spouted about the Gordon men.

"So you can buy the store sooner than you thought," Drusie concluded. "You won't have to wait for me to earn the money. Oh, Gladdie, this is wonderful news!"

"And you know what this means, don't you?"

"Sure. We can get married now, just like you said."

"Yes, it does mean that," Gladdie agreed. "And somethin' else."

The smile disappeared from Drusie's face, replaced by curiosity. "What?"

"It means that you don't have to go to Raleigh after all. You can stay here and sing your sweet little heart out for me."

"Oh." Drusie dropped her hands from his.

"No!" Clara jumped from her seat in protest. "Drusie, you've got to go."

"But she don't need to go," Gladdie argued with fierceness even he didn't realize he felt. "We have the money for the store now. Don't you see, Clara? That's the only reason Drusie was goin' in the first place.

"You can still go," Gladdie pointed out to Clara. "It's just that Drusie don't need to go no more."

"Yes, she does," Clara whined. "Pa won't let either of us go alone. I've waited all my life for a chance to make good, and now I'm this close." She put her forefinger and thumb a quarter inch apart.

"But Clara," Gladdie objected, "you didn't have no hankerin' to sing for pay before your pa came up with the idea."

"I know it, but now that I have the chance, I really want it. I want it real bad!" Clara exclaimed. "I cain't let anybody stand in my way now."

Clara ran to Drusie and took her by the shoulders. "Oh please, Drusie! You cain't let me down. Say you'll go. It won't be that long. No longer than you planned to start with."

Drusie's eyes lit with helplessness, and her posture slumped. "I don't know—"

"I do! You've got to go," Clara wailed.

Drusie turned to Gladdie. "I don't see no way out of it. You see for yourself how disappointed Clara will be if I cain't go. Not to mention, I'm sure Pa's already signed our contract. Please understand, Gladdie."

"But our plans—"

"I ain't gonna let nothin' happen to our plans," Drusie assured. "But if I don't go, and Clara loses her big chance all because of me, I'll never forgive myself. And if you think about it real hard, you know years from now you'll never forgive yourself, either, if you keep Clara from goin'."

Gladdie tried not to glance at Clara, who no doubt would send him a mournful look if he did. He knew he wouldn't be able to stand it. "I don't like this," he murmured.

"I know," Drusie agreed. "Look at it this way. We can still use the extra money to set up our house. A store don't run itself without money. Why, I can even help you pay back your pa faster."

"I know. But I still don't like it. I don't like it one little bit."

seven

The next day before dawn, after excited and emotional farewells with their family, Clara and Drusie were headed out of the mountains toward the state capital. Drusie looked back at the only home she had ever known until it was out of sight, but Clara kept her focus on the road ahead—and on Archie. Drusie hadn't been surprised when her sister hopped into the front with Archie, leaving her in the back. But she had plenty of room and no desire to sit beside the record producer. Judging from the way Archie and Clara stole glances at each other from time to time, their initial attraction to one another hadn't ebbed.

Lord, help me keep Clara out of trouble.

If only Gladdie's love for her hadn't ebbed. Or had it? Couldn't he have stolen a few moments that morning to see her off?

Gladdie must be powerful mad.

Drusie slumped in her seat. Any excitement she once felt about the adventure had long since drained from her spirit. She could only hope—and pray—that time would heal Gladdie's anger. There was no other man for her. She had to come back to him. The sooner the better.

After they'd covered a few miles of crooked mountain roads, Clara took her attention from Archie long enough to look back at Drusie. "I'm sorry Gladdie didn't show up to say good-bye this mornin'."

"He took off a whole day to see Archie. Cain't expect him to live all the time like he ain't got no work to do." Drusie knew the excuse sounded puny, but she couldn't think of anything better to say.

"Maybe so." Clara's voice sounded unconvincing.

"Oh, it's all my fault," Drusie confessed.

"What's your story, morning glory?" Archie asked.

"Nothin'," Drusie answered.

"Oh, Gladdie got the money for the store from his pa, and now he's in a knot over us goin' with you," Clara explained to Archie. She shifted toward Drusie, draping her arm over the back of the front seat. "But don't you worry about that. Gladdie will come around."

"Sure he will." Archie barely slowed for a curve. "We'll be in salad days sure enough soon, and Gladdie won't regret letting Drusie go." He shrugged and glanced back at Drusie in the rearview mirror. "And if he does, well, you can keep all the money for yourself."

"I reckon that's your way of lookin' at things." Drusie tried to keep her voice from sounding too heavy, even though Archie's words didn't comfort her in the least. What was the use of having money if she couldn't share it with Gladdie?

Unwilling to dissect the past day's events further, Drusie stared out the window. The automobile seemed to fly by houses and trees. As they rode down a wide valley, she noticed that most of the trees in this part of the state were still green. Drusie had been hoping to enjoy the drive to Raleigh. She'd never been so far from home and wanted to see a different part of North Carolina at a pace where she could breathe in its beauty. But the way Archie drove, she wondered if they'd even get to their destination in one piece.

Later they passed the courthouse square in Burlington and followed the railroad line east. The drive lasted hour after hour, but since she was so enamored by the idea of seeing the state and because Archie sped along, the ride almost seemed short.

Before she knew it, they had reached Raleigh.

Streets hummed with people who all seemed to have somewhere important to go. The buildings and houses were so close together compared to where she grew up that Drusie found herself feeling a mite closed in by it all. Many of the houses looked like mansions, but Drusie couldn't imagine being happy in any of them. How could anybody live in town, when some of the yards didn't cover as much as an acre? She held back a shudder. Excitement sparked the air, but Drusie longed for the solitude of home.

In contrast, Clara caught a flying bolt of energy before they passed the welcome sign. "Look at all the people! All the stores! Sunshine Holler sure does look slow after bein' here."

Archie chuckled. "You'll get used to it."

Clara eyed a woman wearing a fine wool coat trimmed in fur and a matching hat. "I hope we get to stay long enough for me to get used to it."

"I'm not sure I ever will." Drusie observed what looked like a near miss between two automobiles. Thankfully Archie's Auburn wasn't one of them.

"Where will we be stayin'?" Clara asked.

Drusie hadn't thought of that. Archie seemed to have the world at his command. His swaggering confidence never let up. Surely he had a plan.

He did. "I let all of my out-of-town canaries stay at Mrs. Smyth's Boardinghouse. She only accepts women boarders. I talked to her last week and told her I might be bringing her another lady. She's just set aside one room. You two don't mind sharing, do you?"

"Of course not," Clara said as Drusie nodded. "We share a room at home."

"Good," Archie quipped, "because you'll be sharing a room on the road, too." He glanced at Clara. "Feel like doing a little shopping before I take you to the boardinghouse?"

"Sure!" Eagerness colored her voice.

"Unless you'd like to grab a bite to eat first."

Clara shook her head. "I'm not hungry."

"Good. We can get started." Archie turned left at the next block.

Drusie noticed that Archie didn't seem to care much about her feelings. But then again, if she cared what boardinghouse they slept at, whether they ate, or what store they shopped at, she could always speak up.

Archie pulled in front of a store. ROSE'S FINERY was painted in lime-colored script on the front glass. "This is where I outfit all my stars. She keeps some inventory on hand for me, and she'll alter any dress you like to fit."

Clara clapped her hands, reminding Drusie of when she got a coveted doll for her sixth birthday. "A dress! I get a new dress already?"

He sent her an indulgent smile. "Maybe even two."

They headed into the shop, and moments later, Clara held up a red dress with silver and gold sequins sewn on the bodice. "I love it! Isn't it beautiful?"

Drusie inspected the garment. "I don't know. Isn't it a little low cut?"

"It won't show nothin'. I wouldn't wear nothin' I wouldn't want Grandpappy to see me in."

Rose, a gray-haired woman whose appearance hinted at youthful beauty, chimed in, "Your grandfather would be proud of you in this." She swept her hand in a motion toward racks of attention-getting clothes fit for any stage. "Any of my dresses here would do you proud." She aimed her forefinger at Archie. "That reminds me, Elmer's shirt is ready."

"Good. I'll see that he gets it."

"Will he need another one since you'll be on the road?"

"Not yet. But I might have to place an order for a new band member. That is, if I decide to hire a skin tickler," Archie mused.

"A skin tickler?" Clara asked.

Archie chuckled. "That's a drummer. I think you girls would sound fine with a harmonica and maybe a second fiddle. Even bass. I've got a man in mind who's good on bass and harmonica."

Clara took her gaze from the dress and concentrated on Archie. "You mean, there's gonna be some men in the NC Mountain Girls Band?"

"Well, yes. But you two will be the stars. How could I have two beautiful girl singers onstage and not make them the center of attention?" Archie asked. "Especially if you'll be wearing that pretty dress, Clara."

Clara giggled and held up the dress. "You like it?"

"Looks good on the rack. How's about letting me see you in it? And you try on a dress, too, Drusie. If I'm fronting you canaries the money to buy these dresses, I think I'm entitled to see if they look good."

The last thing Drusie wanted was to let Archie ogle her in a fancy dress, but she realized he had a point. Rose had promised to alter the dresses if they didn't fit, and once they were on the road, sewing wouldn't be easy.

Moments later, each sister emerged in a sparkling frock.

Archie let out a low whistle. "You two look sweet. Not doggy at all."

"I agree!" Rose said with the eagerness of a clerk wanting to close a sale. She tugged at the sash on Clara's waist. "Looks like a perfect fit for you." She inspected the shoulders and waist on Drusie's frock. "You, too." Rose shook her head in disbelieving admiration. "You girls have perfect figures. You're lucky."

"I don't know about luck," Drusie observed. "We just do the

best we can with what God gave us."

"And a fine job you do at that," Archie quipped.

Clara twirled. "I've never felt so wonderful as I do right at this moment."

"This is nothing. Just wait until you're onstage with adoring crowds applauding your every note." He nodded to the store-keeper. "How's about another one for Clara, Rose? Oh, and Drusie, too."

Rose's eyes shone. "I have just the thing. A gold gown with sequins in neat little rows all along the skirt and sleeves."

"Sequins! They look fine on Clara, but for me?" Drusie hadn't given such a daring choice any thought. "I don't know. What do you think, Clara?"

"Oh, I would love for all my gowns to have sequins!"

Rose stood back and admired her handiwork. "They do show up well onstage."

"But do I have to be all sequined?" Drusie scrunched her nose.

Archie chuckled. "I thought you'd like to dress pretty."

Drusie shook her head and watched her sister try on one fancy dress after another. Clara enjoyed every moment of seeing herself and being admired in different outfits. Drusie settled for the only two she tried, happy to have those.

Later, Clara clutched her dress box to her chest as they rode to the boardinghouse. She wouldn't even let Archie put the dresses in the trunk of the car, saying she didn't want to let them out of her sight.

"I've never seen you so excited," Drusie commented.

"I've never been so excited. You don't seem thrilled at all, but I'm not gonna let that spoil my fun."

"Enjoy the fun all you like, because it won't last long. Now we have to work," Archie said. "First thing tomorrow morning we're going to the studio and record your songs."

2a

Gladdie counted six pickled eggs that Mrs. Cunningham ordered, but his mind wasn't on his task. If only he hadn't let Drusie leave without telling her good-bye. He missed her, and the way they left things so uncertain left him longing to see her again. He wanted nothing more than to straighten everything out with her, to kiss her lips again, and to murmur into her ear how much he still wanted to marry her. But he couldn't. At least, not yet.

He handed the customer a mason jar containing the eggs. "Will there be anything else, Mrs. Cunningham?"

She ignored her child's plea for penny candy and counted the eggs. "Yes. One more egg."

Embarrassed, he took the jar she handed him and recounted them. "There sure is one missin'. I'm sorry."

"Sorry that Drusie's left, aren't ya? Cain't concentrate on a thing?" The matron's voice poured out in a sympathetic tone.

"Word does get around." He was glad the task of retrieving one more egg kept him from having to look at her.

"Yep. Fast around this place. Well, I hope she comes back. I'm sure she won't find no other man." One of the Cunningham tots pulled on her skirt. Mrs. Cunningham smiled and grabbed her package. "Put that on my bill."

"Yes, ma'am."

As she hurried out, Gladdie scratched a figure onto the ledger. He wished Mrs. Cunningham hadn't made such a suggestion. He hadn't thought that Drusie might start looking at city slickers with new eyes now that he'd been so mean to her.

Drusie, what have I done?

2a

The sisters spent a comfortable night at Mrs. Smyth's large house, yet sadness permeated Drusie. The reality of her decision had made itself evident. Now she'd give anything for a chance to turn back the clock just a few days, before big ideas about making money for Gladdie to buy the store got into her head. Then she'd still be home, planning to marry Gladdie. She would have been plenty happy no matter what, as long as she was Mrs. Gladdie Gordon. Now she was all alone, living a life she wasn't sure she wanted. And she had no one to blame but herself.

Soon Drusie was distracted by Archie's arrival. Clara brightened in his presence, but all Drusie could see was a long day of work ahead. In no time at all, Archie drove Clara and her into town and parked in front of a nondescript storefront. The tiny, dark studio was nothing like Drusie had imagined. Judging from Clara's lack of a smile, Drusie guessed she was disappointed in the dingy surroundings, too.

Still, the session ran without a hitch. Elmer, a fiddler, looked suave in his cowboy hat. The harmonica player, Al, was a dumpy man who showed them pictures of his children. The musicians seemed pleasant enough, and their demeanor soothed Drusie. Elmer and Al knew all the tunes Archie suggested, and after repeated practice, he deemed them harmonious enough to record. They were to play the song three times all the way through. Archie would make wax recordings of each set and decide later which was the best "take" to produce.

The sisters recorded an old ballad on one side and a gospel tune on the other.

"Good work! Like eggs in coffee." Archie rubbed his palms together. "You'll sound like a million bucks on the radio."

"The radio!" Suddenly Drusie felt nervous. She hadn't considered that people would be listening to them on the radio. All those faceless people sitting in front of boxes in their houses, playing music. What would they think of the NC Mountain Girls?

"Sure you'll be on the radio. How else will people get to know your music? Except for touring, of course. And you'll be singing on live radio, too. Our timing couldn't be better. You'll be joining our tour with the Country Bills and the Sweet Carolinas." Archie looked triumphant.

Clara jumped up and down. "How excitin'!"

For the first time in memory, Drusie wished she had failed. If they hadn't sounded good, then Archie would have sent them home. Against her will, Drusie remembered the other girls back home, with their covetous glances sent Gladdie's way. Sure, he loved only Drusie, but in her absence, would they try awfully hard to convince him to change his mind? Swallowing, she wished more than ever she could go home.

Gladdie, what have I done?

eight

A couple of days later, a caravan of cars met in front of Archie's house to hit the road for the first leg of the tour. The three groups formed a show. They had scheduled performances at radio stations, high school auditoriums, and churches in North Carolina towns. Drusie could only hope she'd be traveling slowly enough to observe the scenery. At least the first day looked hopeful with crystal blue skies and clouds that reminded her of the cotton puffs she kept on her dresser at home.

After suitcases and musical equipment were loaded into automobile trunks, Archie introduced the sisters to the members of the other bands, people they hadn't met during rehearsals. They had already met Al and Elmer, who would be playing backup for all of them. Homer, Orville, and Buford, the trio that called themselves the Country Bills, greeted them kindly but dismissed Clara and Drusie almost as soon as they were introduced. The two young women they approached afterward were a different story.

"June and Betty, I'd like you to meet Drusie and Clara." Archie nodded toward a voluptuous woman whose hair was dyed almost white. "They're part of the Sweet Carolinas."

Clara stood close to Archie. A little too closely, apparently. Drusie saw June's painted eyes shooting daggers at Clara, but Clara seemed too excited by the day's promise to notice.

"How long will you be tourin' with us, honey?" June asked Clara.

"As long as Archie says." Clara gazed at Archie with the adoring look of a schoolgirl fawning over a favored teacher.

"I hope you can keep up," June noted. "Archie works us all right hard. Don't you, Archie?"

Drusie sensed that June was trying to get some hidden message across to Archie, but he didn't seem to notice. He didn't seem to notice much of anything except how to get them going with as much efficiency as possible. With such a businesslike demeanor, Archie hardly seemed intent on intrigue, romantic or otherwise. Drusie could only pray she had misinterpreted June's hard attitude toward Clara.

&

Several days later, the caravan had traveled deep into tobacco country, although the fields lay bare since the leaves had long since been harvested. They had already performed five nights, twice on Saturday, and that night they were scheduled to perform at the county high school and had stopped at a motel on Route 1 long enough to dress before heading out to the school.

"Clara, have you seen my necklace?" Drusie asked.

"What necklace?" Clara responded.

"The gold chain Gladdie gave me. You know, the one with the little heart pendant."

"Oh, that. I don't know how anybody can lose anything, with us bein' more cramped than sardines in a tin."

"At least in this cottage, we ain't sharin' walls with anybody else."

Clara scrunched her nose. "True. In some of the places we stayed, I learned more than I ever wanted to about my band mates, hearin' every conversation through the walls." Combing her hair, she sighed. "I wish we was stayin' in better places."

"This ain't as high on the hog as you imagined, huh?" Drusie rifled through the compartments in her suitcase for the umpteenth time, hoping she might have missed her necklace. "Well, we ain't big stars that can waste money on highfalutin hotel rooms yet. Might never be."

"I don't know. People seem to like us right good. And Archie says he's happy with us." A dreamy look covered her expression. "Archie says after we finish up this tour, we might travel to even more places!"

"Imagine!" Drusie shut her suitcase. "I wonder where that necklace could be?" Her tone sounded as desperate as she felt.

"I don't see how you lost it since you never take it off."

"I do have to take it off when I bathe—and when we perform since it don't go with them fancy dresses you and Archie picked out."

Clara shrugged. "Maybe the clasp came open and you didn't realize it fell off. I'm sure it'll turn up."

"I don't see how I could have misplaced somethin' that important."

"There's no time to look for it now. We've got to be at the automobile in ten minutes." Clara set her comb in her purse and checked her reflection.

"You don't need to stare at yourself in the mirror all the time. You always look good," Drusie assured her.

Clara surveyed her sister. "You should look in the mirror more. Your lipstick is crooked."

Drusie inspected herself. Indeed, one corner of her mouth did appear a bit higher than the other. "I hate this old face paint. I cain't get used to it. And it feels so funny to have a coatin' of stuff on my lips all the time."

Clara laughed. "I kind of like it. This is the only time I can wear face paint without Pa callin' me a harlot."

"I don't know how crazy he'd be about us wearin' paint at all, even to sing. Maybe especially to sing. I wish Archie didn't insist."

"It's just part of the business, Drusie."

"I'll be glad when this tour is over."

"I won't. I could go on like this forever."

They heard a rap on the dressing room door before June entered. "Archie says we gotta get a move on if we want to start the show on time."

"We're almost ready." Drusie decided to grab at the proverbial straw. "Hey, you ain't seen my pendant necklace by chance, have you? The one I wear all the time?"

June's gaze traveled to the hollow of Drusie's neck. "Sure haven't. You lost it?"

"Naw," Clara quipped, "she's just askin' dumb questions to see who'll give the smartest answer."

"Now, Clara," Drusie admonished her sister. As she turned her attention back to June, she saw her make a face at Clara but decided to ignore such schoolgirl antics. "I sure did lose it, and I'd be grateful if you could let me know if you see it anywhere. Can you ask Betty for me, too?"

"Sure thing. But right now, we'd better hustle unless we want Archie to dock our pay." She shut the door behind her.

"She took your necklace! I just know it." Clara snapped shut her compact.

"Oh, pshaw. I know you don't like June since she's got eyes for Archie—"

"So you noticed, huh?" Clara wrinkled her nose. "She hangs on to him like a cheap suit, but he don't pay her no mind."

Drusie blew out a breath. "You ain't here to make enemies. You're here to sing. Try to remember that. And remember somethin' else. Just because you don't like her none don't mean she's a thief."

"I know. I almost wish she was. Then Archie would have an excuse to kick her off the tour."

"You don't want that to happen. We're not famous enough to be headliners yet. We ain't able to fill an auditorium by ourselves."

Clara sniffed. "Well, maybe I can put up with her, then.

Someday I'll be even more famous than her. I'm already prettier."

Drusie would have admonished Clara if she didn't know her sister well enough to realize she spoke at least partly in jest. She shook her head and watched Clara admire herself in the looking glass. She was definitely enjoying her newfound celebrity and the attention she gleaned from it. Watching Clara apply a fresh coat of red lip rouge, Drusie felt led to pray that Clara wouldn't let fame carry her astray.

ↄ

The week drew to a close, but no break was in sight for the tour. To Drusie, it seemed Archie had booked them in every town and venue possible. They were getting well known, though, and Archie said their record sales were up.

That wasn't all that was up. Drusie had caught Archie giving Clara a quick kiss on the lips, supposedly for good luck. The gesture had left Clara so disoriented that once they were performing, Drusie had to guide her through the second chorus of "When God Dips His Pen of Love in My Heart," a song they had sung since they were girls.

Drusie's feelings about Archie and Clara forming a bond were mixed. On the one hand, despite the age difference of a few years, they seemed to get along well, and she could see them working side by side as a married couple, in love with music and with each other. On the other hand, there was June. Jealousy sparked in her eyes whenever Clara entered the room. Even though she'd never seen Archie and June in any exchange that didn't involve business, Drusie had a feeling Archie was pushing June aside for Clara. She could only pray that Archie's feelings toward her sister were true and that the turnabout in romantic inclinations was part of God's plan. She didn't like June much, but she didn't want to see her heart broken, either. Drusie kept them all in her prayers.

෨

Gladdie swept the floor of Goode's Mercantile with energetic motions.

"You keep on like that and we'll have us a dust storm," Mr. Goode observed from behind the counter.

"I'm sorry. I'll try to be more gentle." He slowed his pace, knowing that he had gotten caught up in thoughts of the future and had started sweeping too rapidly as a result. He didn't want to admit how he couldn't wait for the day when Mr. Goode's name would be replaced with his own.

The shop bell tinkled, signaling the arrival of a new customer. Gladdie looked and saw two men he didn't know. They were dressed in the same style of suit that Archie wore. Tourists from out of town, no doubt.

He propped his broom against the counter and swiped his hands against his trousers legs. "Mornin', gentlemen. What might I help you with today?"

"Nothing, Gladdie," Mr. Goode said. "They're here to see me."

"Oh!" Gladdie retrieved his broom faster than a fly escaping a swatter. "Sorry," he muttered.

Mr. Goode tilted his head toward the men but kept his gaze on Gladdie. "We've got some business to tend to, son, so I'll be taking my friends across the street to the diner."

"Yes, sir." Gladdie wondered what could be so important that Mr. Goode, never one to spend an extra dime, would be treating strangers to lunch.

Mr. Goode eyed the display of sewing notions. "Now you go on and hold down the fort here. And in between customers, hows about you making sure the buttons are sorted? The Billings girls were playing in them today, and I suspect they misplaced some."

"Yes, sir."

Mr. Goode smiled and addressed his visitors. "He's a mighty fine worker, that one is."

"Looks like it," one of the men agreed. "He seems to be an asset for you."

Mr. Goode didn't comment but rushed the men out. Gladdie wondered why he never introduced his friends from out of town.

⁂

An hour before the show, Archie rapped on the dressing room door. "Drusie! Telephone for you. Long distance."

She stopped powdering her face. "Long distance!"

"Long distance?" Clara echoed with equal surprise. "I hope nothin's wrong at home."

"Me, too."

"Don't blow your wig," Archie cautioned. "Just go to the business office and take the call. Then you'll have your answer."

"You have a point," Drusie conceded and hurried to the office. Archie showed her the telephone that was almost lost amid papers and a cup of coffee that still left its scent in the room. She picked up the heavy black receiver. "Hello?"

"Drusie?"

She could barely hear the disembodied voice that sounded like it came from another world, but the sweet tone was recognizable to her ears. "Gladdie! Is that you?"

"Sure is. You sound mighty winded. You okay?"

"Sure I am. I just had to run from my dressin' room to the auditorium's business office."

"Oh. I've been tryin' to reach you for several days now, but I couldn't never catch up with you. Y'all are movin' right fast through the countryside."

"We sure are. Is everything all right? I know this telephone call is costin' plenty. You callin' from the store?"

"Sure am."

"Mr. Goode will be dockin' your wages when the bill comes, then."

"I know it. But it's worth it," he assured her.

"Is everybody okay? Have you seen Ma and Pa?"

"They're just fine. Your ma was in the store yesterday, buyin' rickrack. I told her I'd be talkin' to you soon."

She leaned against the wooden desk. "Tell Ma and Pa I love 'em and miss 'em. Will you do that for me?"

"Sure will." He paused. "Drusie, I'm sorry about the way we left things."

She didn't hesitate. "Me, too."

"Really?"

"Really. I've been prayin' about it. You know, I wish I was there instead of here."

"I should've come to say good-bye to you the mornin' you left. I'll never let anything like that happen again."

"That's all in the past." She sighed. "I never should've gotten so greedy and gotten such big ideas in my head."

"You weren't greedy. You were just tryin' to help me. And I'll always love you for that."

Touched, she figured he planned to end the call there. But an intake of his breath told her otherwise.

"Will you come home as soon as the tour's over?"

"That's my plan."

"You won't let them city slickers charm you too much, will you?"

Drusie laughed. "City slickers? What gave you such a silly notion?"

"Oh, nothin'."

"Seen Edna Sue around lately?" she couldn't resist asking.

"She's been in the store once or twice. Why?"

Puzzlement in his tone and his nonchalant answer assured Drusie that if Edna Sue had set her sights on Gladdie in a big way, he still wasn't paying her any mind. "Just wondered."

"Oh, Bertha and Gertie said to tell you hello. They miss you in Sunday school class."

"I miss them, too."

"Drusie?"

"Yes?"

"I'd like it a powerful lot if you'd write to me."

She smiled into the receiver. "I will from now on, every day."

"I'll wait for the postman to come every day, then," he promised. "I love you, Drusie."

"I love you, too, Gladdie."

When she hung up, Drusie knew that once again all was right with her world.

The good feeling was shattered by Clara's scream.

nine

Drusie ran in the direction of the shriek and soon entered the door of their dressing room. Clara stood in front of her favorite dress that hung on a rack, waiting to be donned for the performance. Archie and Elmer hovered in the background, also having responded to Clara's cry of distress.

"What's wrong?" they all asked.

Clara picked up the hem of her red dress and held out the skirt for them to examine. "Look." Her voice caught on that one word, and Drusie realized that her sister could utter no more.

As soon as she viewed the skirt, Drusie could see why Clara had screamed. Holes about a half inch in diameter, encircled by brown rings, marred the fabric. "Looks like somebody burned your skirt with a cigarette."

Archie viewed the damage. "Whoever did this didn't just burn the dress. It's been attacked—viciously. There are even holes in the top."

Clara let go of the hem and wailed. "I cain't possibly wear this."

Archie groaned. "All that money down the drain."

Drusie suspected June was the culprit, but speculation would do them no good this close to showtime. She did note that June was nowhere around. No doubt she had busied herself with a fictitious errand so she wouldn't be nearby when Clara discovered the deed.

Clara dabbed a handkerchief at her eyes in an obvious attempt to keep tears from destroying the face paint she had applied. "My beautiful dress! What am I gonna do?"

"Simple. Wear the other one," Archie suggested. "You look beautiful in them both."

Clara nodded and took the other dress out of its garment bag. When they saw holes in that dress, too, everyone let out a gasp. This time Clara didn't bother to catch her tears. They streamed down her face.

Archie took her in a loose embrace. Drusie couldn't help but notice that the gesture didn't seem romantic. With witnesses, no doubt Archie planned it that way. "That's okay, doll. I'll buy you another dress."

"You can borrow mine tonight," Drusie said.

Clara brightened. "I—I can?" Just as quickly her smile evaporated. "But Drusie, you don't have but one dress, do you?"

Drusie remembered that she had dropped off her green dress at a local seamstress's shop to have a ribbon reattached. The shop had long since closed. "That's okay. You can wear the fancy dress. I'll just wear what I've got on." She looked down at her red gingham dress. While clean, flattering, and serviceable, the frock didn't compare to anything with sequins.

"That won't look right, with one of you in sequins and the other in something so plain," Archie said.

"I don't care." Drusie's voice came out with more defiance than she intended. "We ain't gonna let nobody get us down. Somebody don't want Clara to go out there in her good dress, and she's just about succeeded. But I don't care if I have to wear rags—Clara's gonna look like a million bucks." Drusie crossed her arms and rooted her foot to make herself look as rigid as possible.

"You said 'she,'" Archie noticed. "You think you know who did this?"

"I have an idea—June," Clara said.

"June?" Archie laughed. "I don't think she'd do that."

"You don't, do you?" Elmer guffawed. "Then you don't know much about women, Archie. She's been madder than a bull in a pen ever since you brought Clara here."

Archie shot Elmer a dirty look. "Aw, June must have caught us in a honey cooler."

"Honey cooler?" Drusie queried.

Archie shuffled his foot. "You know—a kiss."

"So there's been more than one?" Drusie blurted.

"Never mind that." Clara's cheeks blazed, a sure sign that "honey coolers" had been the rule of the day with them.

Drusie wished she had kept a closer eye on her sister, but if Clara was determined to kiss Archie, Drusie could do little to stop her.

"Before we got here, were you and June a couple?" Clara asked Archie.

"No. As far as I'm concerned, she's just another canary."

Drusie turned to Elmer. "Do you think June had reason to think otherwise?"

"Aw, you see how women act around Archie. He draws the ladies like bees to honey. But I never saw him treat June different from anybody else. And if you don't believe me, I'll swear on the Bible."

"You don't have to go that far, Elmer," Drusie said. "Archie, you better not be playin' my sister for a fool."

"I'm not. I swear. You can bring me a Bible, too, if you want."

Drusie discerned more from Archie's plaintive expression and clear tone of voice than from his willingness to swear on the Bible. "Okay. But if you are, you'll be answerin' to our pa."

"Considering what a good shot he is with that rifle of his, I know I don't want to cross him." Archie's half grin conveyed levity, but Drusie knew he was serious. He drew his watch from his pocket and glanced at its face. "It's getting late. Elmer and I had better take a powder so you girls can get dressed."

With that, the men exited.

Clara gave Drusie a light embrace. "I'll never forget you for doin' this."

"I hope you'll never forget me anyway," Drusie joked.

Clara's gaze met Drusie's. "Are you mad at me for not tellin' you about Archie and me?"

"You was afraid I'd tell Pa and you'd have to go home, warn't you?"

"I was. Are you gonna tell him? Archie said if he found out, that would be the end of the tour."

"I don't care half as much about this tour as I care about you. Do you really think Archie loves you?" Drusie searched her sister's face. "I know we all grew up together, but Archie is a little older than you, and as adults you haven't known each other all that long."

"I do think Archie loves me. I—I know he does. But you know somethin'—I cain't think about marryin' him until his heart softens toward the Lord more. I think he got mad at God for takin' his parents so long ago, and he ain't been back to the Lord since."

"Nothin's too big to handle with God's help, but I can understand why a little boy would get mad and confused over such tragedy. But he's a grown man now, and it's high time he changed his outlook." Drusie stared at the wall but didn't think about the faded yellow paint. She could only feel sadness at Archie's loss and say a quick, silent prayer that his heart would change. Her prayer led her to express an idea. "Clara, maybe you can be the one to lead him back to God."

"I've thought of that." Clara looked down at her skirt. "And I've thought of somethin' else. I cain't kiss him anymore unless I plan to marry him. It just ain't right."

Drusie sent her sister a knowing smile. "I'm glad Ma and Pa don't have to be here for you to know right from wrong.

I know if God wants you and Archie to be together, you will be. . .someday."

"I wouldn't tell this to nobody else, but I hope so. He hinted that he'd like to marry me someday, but I didn't do nothin' to take him up on his offer."

Drusie moved to give her sister a hug. "It'll all work out. You'll see. Now come on. We got a show to do."

Onstage later, Drusie couldn't help but feel self-conscious as she appeared in gingham while her sister shone in sequins. She surveyed the audience, even though she wasn't able to see much with spotlights flooding the stage and the people watching them sitting in relative darkness. She did eye a brunette in fur. The woman had been following them lately. She seemed to brighten whenever the men took to the stage. Drusie held back a smile. The men attracted quite a few female admirers.

Without meaning to, Drusie wondered how many male fans came to see them. She was glad she would never have to find out. Archie made sure they were protected from any bold men who might have been looking for more than an autograph.

Clara took to the spotlight like a duck to water. She couldn't remember when her sister had sung with a voice as pure and sweet. Clearly, onstage life suited her. She always approached each new performance with anticipation. Drusie, on the other hand, felt dread. Singing for the folks at home—her friends and family—was one thing. Entertaining strangers made her nervous.

Maybe I should let her be the star all the time.

Drusie made a point of observing June, who sat with her partner, Betty, along with the Country Bills, as they awaited their turn. At first the blond wore a triumphant grin when Drusie took to the stage in her plain dress. June's mouth turned into a red slash as soon as Clara appeared in her stage attire. June puffed with more vigor on her cigarette and glared at her competition. Yes, June was the culprit.

An unpleasant thought occurred to Drusie. She had no doubt that June was out to cause trouble. Could she have taken her necklace?

&

Gladdie always made a point of arriving a few minutes before the store's opening, a fact Mr. Goode had said time and time again he greatly appreciated. As soon as Gladdie entered, Mr. Goode wasted no time in greeting him. "Gladdie, I've got some news. It's time for us to talk."

"Be right with you, sir." Gladdie hung his coat and hat on their customary hook with as much nonchalance as he could muster, contrary to his shaking hands and rapid heartbeat.

Not one for idle chatter or gossip, Mr. Goode never said he had news unless the message was important. Surely he was about to say that he planned to accept Pa's offer for the store and that Gladdie would soon be the owner. In his mind, he rehearsed one last time how he would assure Mr. Goode that he would do Sunshine Hollow proud and keep up the fine level of quality and service their customers had grown to expect. He still wasn't sure he could promise he wouldn't change the name of the store to reflect his ownership. Surely Mr. Goode would understand Gladdie's desire to tell the world he was finally his own boss.

In an uncustomary move, Mr. Goode sat by the potbellied stove and poured himself a cup of coffee. Normally he'd finished his morning beverage long before Gladdie arrived. "Have a cup?" Mr. Goode asked.

"No thank you, sir. I had plenty at breakfast this mornin'." He didn't want to admit that he couldn't imagine drinking or eating anything at the moment. Anticipation had brightened his spirit but dulled his appetite.

"Sit down, son." Mr. Goode motioned to the empty oak rocker by the stove.

"Yes, sir." He obeyed even though he would rather have stood.

Mr. Goode took a swig of black coffee. "I suppose I might have summoned your pa in here, but I figured you and I could talk like men."

The admission made Gladdie's heart beat faster than ever. The mention of his pa could only mean one thing—that the store would soon be his. "I can relay whatever message Pa needs to hear. He knows he can trust me."

"I know it." The elder man took another swig slowly. A little too slowly.

Gladdie wondered why he was so reticent to relay welcome news. *Maybe he's just now realizin' how sad he'll be to leave the store forever.*

Mr. Goode cleared his throat. "I reckon you recall that not too long ago, a couple of men came here to the store and we all went out to lunch."

"Yes, sir. They were dressed in nice suits, the kind like my cousin Archie wears."

"I know they didn't look like they belonged here in these parts, and there's a good reason for that. They don't. They were here from out of town on business." He paused.

"Business?" A sick feeling visited the pit of Gladdie's stomach.

"Yep. They were representin' some buyers from out of town. Buyers of the store."

"Oh." Gladdie didn't know what to say. Surely Mr. Goode wouldn't sell the store out from under him. Not when he knew how much he wanted to go into business for himself. Yet when Mr. Goode stopped looking at him, Gladdie knew what had happened. He had accepted their offer.

"Gladdie, I know you and your pa thought I'd sell to you, and if you want to know the truth, I'd planned to. But none of us shook hands on the deal, so when this other offer came in, I had to take it."

"They're payin' a powerful lot of money, ain't they?" Gladdie's voice registered just above a whisper.

Mr. Goode nodded. "More than I know you and your pa could ever pay."

"But why? I mean, this here store is swell for Sunshine Holler, but it don't make enough money to impress people from out of town. Does it?"

"Well, they said that the people they represent want to live here now. They love the mountains and they have family here."

"What family?"

"I don't rightly know." Mr. Goode shrugged. "I reckon all will be clear before you know it."

Gladdie tried to digest what the storekeeper said, but disappointment clouded his reasoning. All he could do was fight back bitterness and anger. He tensed his hands against the chair rails to keep them from balling up into fists.

Mr. Goode leaned forward in his seat. "You know I think of you like a son, but I had to take the money. My daughter in Raleigh ain't rich, and she'll need whatever the sale of the store brings for the two of us to live. Trust me, she's grateful. And so am I."

"I understand," Gladdie forced himself to answer.

"I did look out for you. I told them you're a mighty fine clerk and that the new owners would be powerful foolish not to keep you on."

"Thank you." Gladdie knew the tone of his voice was like that of a little boy who'd gotten a doll for Christmas instead of a bike, but he couldn't muster much gratitude, try as he might.

"I know this is a disappointment for you and your family, and I'm sorry about that. But at least you still have a job. I'm sure they'll keep you on. And in these tough times, a job is somethin' to be grateful for." Mr. Goode finished his coffee and stood. "Now let's get to work."

Gladdie knew he'd seen all the sentiment Mr. Goode would be able to summon. He had to follow his orders. Having to tell Pa that Mr. Goode had sold the store out from under them was bad enough; he didn't want to tell him he'd lost his job, too. When he heard the news, Gladdie imagined Pa would call Mr. Goode a snake, but other than harbor ill will, there was nothing they could do. Nothing. And Gladdie knew the Bible forbade them even the luxury of hard feelings.

"Forgive us our trespasses, as we forgive those who trespass against us."

Yes, he would have to forgive Mr. Goode whether he wanted to or not. And he would. Surely Pa would, too. . .given time.

For once Gladdie felt glad Drusie was on tour. He wasn't ready to tell her yet that they'd have to find a different way to make good in Sunshine Hollow.

❧

"You girls sure pleased the crowd tonight," Archie praised Drusie and Clara after the show.

"Oh, Archie! Each show is even more excitin' than the last one," Clara proclaimed, looking up into his face. "I never get tired of singin' for a crowd."

"You wouldn't be just telling me that now, would you?"

"Oh no! I really mean it!"

Archie laughed. "I know you do. I was just jesting."

Elmer chose that moment to enter. " 'Scuse me for interrupting, but Al's feelin' mighty poorly. He don't look so good, either."

"I thought he looked a mite peaked this evenin'," Drusie observed.

Archie scowled. "He's been telling me he's under the weather, but I hoped he could hold on. I don't need him dropping out and gumming up the works."

"He cain't help it if he's sick," Drusie pointed out.

"Yeah, I know. Elmer, have you called a doctor?"

Elmer nodded. "There was a doctor in the house, and he says Al needs to go home. He's got pneumonia."

"Pneumonia!" Drusie said. "This is terrible!"

"You said it!" Archie blurted. "Elmer, can you see to it that Al's taken to the hospital? I'll get everyone here rounded up and see if I can figure out a way to get another harmonica player."

"Will we have to cancel the tour if we cain't find anybody?" Clara asked.

"No, but your sound really changes without a harmonica. Wonder who we can get now?"

Drusie didn't hesitate. "Gladdie is a great harmonica player."

"He sure is!" Clara confirmed.

"That's swell, but doesn't he work at a store?" Archie asked.

"Yes, but I can ask him what he thinks of joinin' us," Drusie offered. "He knows every song Clara and I sing even better than we do."

"I won't argue with you on that." Clara twisted a stray curl. "But won't that interfere with Mr. Goode trainin' him to take over?"

"Well, that's not a done deal yet," Drusie admitted. "The last time we talked over the telephone, Gladdie said that Mr. Goode listened to the offer he and his pa made, but he ain't accepted it as of yet. But once the store's sold, Gladdie will be tied to it right good. So I have a notion that him takin' a little break to join our tour for a week or two may be just the thing for all concerned."

"Snazzy," Archie said. "We can stay put while we get you girls new dresses and wait for Gladdie to catch up with us. If we play our cards right, we can make up the time on the road without havin' to cancel a performance. I can let the radio station know we need to perform in the afternoon instead of morning."

All that planning made Drusie dizzy, but she could see that Archie had confidence in what he said.

Archie directed his attention to Drusie. "Why don't you use the telephone in the office to call Gladdie first thing tomorrow? You should be able to catch him at the store."

#

"You told Drusie you'd do what?" Gladdie's father was so taken aback that some of the slop missed the pig trough.

Gladdie made sure to be more careful with his bucket. He didn't need Pa fussing at him about the pig slop on top of everything else. At least he'd thought far enough ahead to break the news to Pa while they were busy with chores. With bucket in hand, Pa couldn't throttle him.

If he was going to be a man, he had to act like one. Straightening himself, he looked Pa in the eye. "I told Drusie I'm joinin' the band as a harmonica player. Don't worry. I won't run off and marry her or nothin'. I'll be a gentleman like all the Gordon men are."

"I ain't worried about that. I wonder if you're just runnin' away from your problems now that the store cain't be yours."

"I ain't tryin' to run away, Pa. I admit that nothin's been the same since I found out Mr. Goode took a better offer, but I wouldn't run away. Maybe the timin' of this whole thing with the band is God's doin'."

The two men headed for the gate, and Gladdie held it open for his pa. The men were quick to exit before any pigs took a notion to escape.

"So you cleared this with Goode already?"

"Yes, sir."

"And he didn't mind?"

"No, sir. I think he knows in his heart he done wrong. Or not exactly right, anyway."

Pa stopped so short that the bucket hit against his leg, but he didn't seem to notice. "Wonder who this mystery family is?" He snorted. "Probably them Moores."

"Hard to say, but I'd like to think they wouldn't do such a thing." Gladdie shrugged. "I reckon we'll find out from Zeb."

"Zeb? What's your brother got to do with this? I know he don't care nothin' for cipherin' and all the other work that goes along with keepin' shop."

"No, but he did say he'd like to take my place as clerk until I get back. I hope that's okay with you. Is it, Pa?"

They had reached the barn, and Pa motioned for Gladdie's bucket so he could store both containers in their proper places until feeding time rolled around again. "I reckon so. You boys have to make your way in the world, and I have to get used to the fact I cain't hold you here forever."

❧

A few days after Drusie placed the long-distance call to him, Gladdie caught up with the band. As soon as she spotted the familiar figure she loved emerging from a bus, Drusie ran to him. "Gladdie! I didn't think you'd ever get here!"

"It was a long ride, but here I am." He set down his suitcase and enveloped her in his arms.

His lips met hers in a kiss that seemed to melt the frigid air around them. Old feelings reawakened, their ardor reminding her all the more how much she had yearned to be near Gladdie and how glad she was that he had finally arrived.

"Enough, you two. We all know you're dizzy with this dame," Archie teased. "Need help with that bag, Gladdie?"

Gladdie broke the embrace slowly enough to let Drusie know he was sorry for the interruption. "Nope. I got it."

Archie started walking to the car. "Too bad you won't be

seeing much of North Carolina. We're heading into Virginia and Tennessee on the next leg of the tour."

Gladdie picked up his bag and followed, along with Drusie. "Anywhere else?" he asked.

"Maybe Kentucky. Anywhere our music will be well received. This tour has helped get the girls known. Before long, we'll all be rich."

Gladdie touched Drusie's shoulder. "The longer you were gone from me, the less I cared about being rich. And I still don't care nothin' about havin' more than I need. I'm just glad we're together now."

"You'll be sick enough of each other with all the rehearsals and performances we have scheduled," Archie jested as he opened the trunk of his Auburn. "Gladdie, you need to run through the music with the band tonight and work in your part."

Gladdie tossed in his suitcase. "Fine. Has the other harmonica player gotten over what ails him?"

"He'll recover, but not before this tour is over."

"I'm sorry to hear it's gonna take so long for him to get well. I hate that my opportunity came at someone else's expense."

Archie shrugged. "I know it. But that's life."

"I reckon. Say, Archie, do you mind if I take Drusie out for a cup of coffee at the diner?" Gladdie cocked his head toward an establishment in sight of them.

Archie nodded. "Sure. There's time. June and Betty have a new number they want to go over, but after that I do need you to rehearse with the band. I know the girls are used to your playing, but Elmer needs to get comfortable with you, and you need to get to know him. Hows about I give you two love birds a half hour?"

"That's not enough, but we'll take it." Gladdie grabbed Drusie's hand, and they headed off for some time alone.

ten

Gladdie looked across the table at Drusie. With her eyes bright in excitement and her elated expression, she looked more beautiful than ever. They'd been apart too long.

A waitress carried a hot, open-faced roast beef sandwich and a ham dinner past them, sending enticing aromas their way. On the counter, slices of pie and pastries looked tempting under glass. He wished they had enough time for dinner, but he also knew Archie had to keep the band members to a schedule if they hoped to perform at the grueling pace he set for them. At least the coffee looked rich and smelled delicious. Sugar and cream added to the brew made for a tasty pick-me-up.

"And you know what?" Drusie was saying. "Archie never could get June to confess to burnin' holes in them dresses. Not that I blame her. He was plannin' to dock her pay—or worse. I just hope she got the idea of revenge out of her system and Archie's threats were enough to stop her."

"Judgin' from what you told me, she's mad as an old sittin' hen, all right. It ain't no fun to be thrown over for someone else."

"How would you know?" she jested.

"I don't know for sure, and I don't want to find out."

"I can tell you one thing; she'll never get to our clothes like that again. And I'm keeping an extra close watch on my money and jewelry."

"Why is that? She don't have nothin' against you, does she? Other than the fact you're Clara's sister."

"No, and I've always been nothin' but nice to her. But. . ." Drusie added an unnecessary spoonful of sugar to her coffee and stirred.

"What's wrong?"

She set her spoon on the plain white saucer that matched the cup. A tear escaped from the corner of her eye. "Oh, I was hopin' I'd find it before you came. I looked and looked and looked. Nothin'."

He knew what she meant. "The gold necklace."

She nodded, and tears came at a rapid pace. "I'm sorry."

He handed her his handkerchief and patted her hand. "Now don't you worry one little bit. I can buy you another necklace. Now that I'm in the band, I can buy you one soon. Maybe even one with a diamond."

"But I don't want a necklace with a diamond. I want the one you already gave me. It means a lot to me."

"You still got me. Now that I'm here with you, you don't need to read 'I love you' engraved on a pendant. I can tell you myself, every day."

She patted her eyes. "Well, that's the best way to look at it, I reckon." She smiled.

"That's better. So you think not only that she burned holes in Clara's dresses, but that June's a thief in your midst, too?"

"It seems maybe so. Things turn up missin' from time to time."

Gladdie finished his coffee and set down the cup. "As much as y'all move around from place to place, it's no wonder things get lost."

"True. I just hope you're right. I have another story that beats that, though. Two weeks ago, a show producer shorted us on ticket receipts."

"That's awful! How can somebody get away with that?"

"Archie tries to line us up with people who'll pay our fee

ahead of time, but it's not always possible, apparently. He says sometimes we get involved with someone that ain't honest. There's not much we can do. At least we were just shorted and they didn't run off with the whole sum of admission money."

"True."

The waitress appeared again, and Gladdie accepted another cup of coffee even though Drusie declined. He wanted to linger and get the bad news out of the way. "Drusie?"

"What is it?"

"I have somethin' to tell you. I'm tellin' you now because I don't think you'll haul off and hit me in front of all these people." He looked around in an exaggerated manner.

"Haul off and hit you? You're a silly old thing. What's the matter?" She leaned across the table.

Her levity eased him. "First of all, I want you to know that I'll always be grateful to you for agreein' to sing in Archie's band so I could buy the store, even if Pa did end up comin' up with the money."

She reached over and took his hand. "I'd do anything for you. Thank you for lettin' me come out here with Clara. You haven't seen her yet, but she's blossomed under the limelight."

"And ain't got into much trouble?" he joked.

"Not too much. She and Archie seem to have found romance."

"They have? Well, how about that." He paused. "Come to think of it, I could sense somethin' in the air with them even before you left. You don't mind her gettin' involved with him, do you?"

"Not if it makes her happy. And after gettin' to know him, I've decided Archie's okay." She smiled. "But we've gotten off the subject, and the waitress is eyein' us like she'd like us to leave so somebody else can have this booth."

Gladdie cut his glance to the waitress. "Yeah. Right. Well, anyway, I've decided I don't want to keep shop all my life."

Drusie gasped. "You don't?"

"That's right."

"I don't believe it."

"I don't blame you. The whole story isn't as simple as all that. You see, the decision has been made for me. Mr. Goode sold the store out from under Pa and me."

"What?"

"That's right." Gladdie filled her in on all the details.

"Maybe the Moores will sell you their store," Drusie joked.

"If only." Gladdie let out a humorless chuckle. "You know what? This ain't what I thought I'd want—being out of a chance to own the store—but maybe it's what God wants. Why else would He let somethin' like that happen?"

"He does let things happen for a reason."

"I believe that, too."

"God works all for good." She squeezed his hand. "And now you're here. With me. Could we ask for more?"

"No. We sure couldn't."

&

Four weeks later, Drusie knew that she had never been happier. For the first time since leaving Sunshine Hollow in Archie's Auburn, she enjoyed rising each morning in anticipation. Seeing Gladdie every day lifted her spirits. She knew she'd missed him while they were apart, but she didn't know just how much until they were together again.

"You look mighty cheerful," Clara noticed as they dressed for yet another performance.

"That's because I am." Drusie wiggled into her costume. "I'm enjoyin' singin' for folks a powerful lot more now that Gladdie's onstage with us. He gives me more confidence in singin' for folks I don't know."

"And I don't?" Clara jested.

"Sure, you help me a lot. More than you know. Sometimes

I don't think I could've made it at all if you hadn't been here. And that's the truth," Drusie said. "And I have to say, I'm not as afraid of audiences as I used to be. I reckon I've gotten used to not knowin' nobody I'm singin' for."

"Not to mention, Archie's rehearsed us so many times I think I'm recitin' lines and singin' in my sleep."

Drusie laughed.

"I know you bein' happier has made Archie happy, too."

"There's only one thing. I'm gettin' tired of wearin' this stiff fabric. It's scratchy, too."

"But so pretty. And you know what Archie says. He says with the Depression on, people like to see singers wearin' pretty clothes even if they cain't afford to buy nice things for themselves."

"Like the men havin' to wear rhinestones and beads on their suits, huh?" Drusie grinned and shook her head. "Could you imagine them wearin' such getups anywhere else but onstage?"

"No, I cain't." Clara touched the hem of her dress. "But I sure do like my dress. It's even prettier than the one June burned."

"Now we cain't go around sayin' that even though we suspect," Drusie scolded. "After all, it ain't happened no more. Looks like whoever did it learned their lesson."

"Maybe, but if it was her, I wish she'd own up to it."

"She won't. The Hays Code might make sure everybody in the movies who's done somethin' wrong gets punished, but we ain't in no motion picture."

"It don't seem right. Why should she get off scot-free?"

Drusie shrugged. "I know it. But the Bible never promised us that everybody who does wrong will be punished here on the earth. She may look like she's gettin' away with somethin', but she ain't. At least, not in the long run."

Clara adjusted her bodice. "I reckon you're right."

"What we need to do now is pray that June finds the right man for her. If Archie was the right man for June, he never woulda looked at you twice."

"True." Clara nodded once. "And because you pointed that out, I think I will pray for her."

Drusie looked at the wall clock. "First we'd better get through this show."

"You're right. Time to get on out there."

Moments later, Drusie stood by Gladdie, waiting to go onstage. She eyed a now-familiar woman and tugged on his sleeve. "Who is that woman?"

He peered into the audience. "What woman?"

"She's sittin' on the second row, near the center. See? She's the brunette wearin' fur."

Gladdie spotted the woman in question. "She sure is familiar. Warn't she in the audience in several places in Tennessee?"

"Yes, and Virginia, too. And now it looks like she's followed us back to North Carolina."

Elmer interrupted. "Who you talkin' about?"

"This woman in the second row. She sure travels a lot," Gladdie said. "She's been followin' the band awhile now. Got any idea who she might be?"

"I—uh, why would you think I know?"

His stammering drew Drusie's attention. "You seem like you're a little slow to answer."

"I told you, I don't know."

Gladdie laughed. "So you say. Is she comin' to see you play every night?"

"You could do worse," Drusie said. "She's mighty pretty."

"Aw, come on. They're all here to see you and Clara. You're the stars."

Approaching from behind, Archie shushed them. "Stop your yammering. You're being introduced."

"He's right. We're on." Gladdie brushed Drusie's lips with his. The gesture never failed to send chills down her spine.

Drusie hung back as the band took to the stage and played a few chords of "Cindy." She and Clara were always introduced after that.

Archie placed his hand on the small of Clara's back and whispered something in her ear. Watching them, Drusie could only hope that he wouldn't break Clara's heart. She wanted her sister to have a real love, a love like she and Gladdie knew.

The rustle of a dress lured her gaze behind the couple. June's expression as she observed Archie and Clara held a mixture of wistfulness and resignation. Drusie had a feeling that June wouldn't be burning holes in any more dresses.

Soon their set was completed, and the sound of applause filled the air. Drusie lingered long enough to hear Gladdie play harmonica for the other bands. His music added texture to any act of which he was part.

She applauded wildly for him.

He met her backstage after the show.

"You thrive under that spotlight, don't you?" she said.

"I hate to admit it, because I don't want to seem like I think I should be the center of attention, but I do enjoy performin' for the crowd a lot more than I ever thought I would."

"That's because they appreciate you. But not as much as I do."

"They appreciate you. You were wonderful tonight. You're wonderful every night." He punctuated the statement with a kiss.

"You were even better." Drusie kissed him back. If only they were married. Traveling together had brought them some temptation they hadn't experienced at home under the vigilant eyes of their parents. Yet they knew they could trust each other. Both were too committed to God and a strong beginning for their marriage to go beyond a kiss.

"I wish we could marry right away," Gladdie mused.

"I know," Drusie agreed. "I wish we could, too. But you know it would break Ma's and Pa's hearts if we didn't marry in the same little church where they were wed all them years ago. And what kind of married life could we have on the road like this, anyway?"

They were interrupted by Archie. "That no good Burns."

"What do you mean?" Gladdie wanted to know. "Who's Burns?"

"Isn't he the show's producer?" Drusie guessed.

"He sure is. Or was—before he disappeared."

"What do you mean, he disappeared?" Drusie felt her heart sink in her chest.

Archie shrugged, a nonchalant motion that defied his face grown red with rage. "He up and left. No one seems to know where he is. At least, they're not willing to tell me."

"He's the stocky man wearing a cowboy hat and boots, right?" Drusie asked.

"Yes, that describes him. Have you seen him?" Archie's eyes took on a hopeful glint.

"Not since before the show. And I don't know where he would have run off to. I saw him takin' the ticket money, so it's not like our show was a flop," Drusie observed. "He—he did pay you our fee before he left, right?"

"That's just it. He didn't," Archie said. "Otherwise, I wouldn't care where he'd run off to."

"Drusie told me somethin' like this happened before." Shadows hovered over Gladdie's face as the stagehands dimmed the lights.

Archie started walking toward the dressing rooms. Drusie and Gladdie followed. "Yeah, but I had it on good word from one of my contacts that this guy could be trusted. I'll remember not to trust him again," Archie said. "I feel awful about it. I try to protect us, but we're out on our own in this world. From now on, our show is not performing for anybody until we're paid. And that's final."

"That's all you can do, Archie," Gladdie agreed.

"I hate having to punish the honest ones because of the ones who aren't so good."

"It's not your fault," Drusie said. "Don't beat yourself up. You do your best. And that's usually pretty good!"

"Yeah," Archie agreed.

Drusie took that as her cue to depart. "I know one thing. I've got to change out of this outfit. I'll let you know if I see Mr. Burns, Archie."

"Oh, one thing before you go," Archie said. "Speaking of seeing things, have either of you seen my mother-of-pearl cuff links?"

Gladdie and Drusie both shook their heads no. "When did you last see 'em?" Gladdie inquired.

"Last night, when I took them off to go to bed. I couldn't find them this morning, so I had to put on these other ones. Good thing I brought an extra set, even if I don't like them half as much." He shook his head. "I can't believe the thief has struck again."

"Maybe you just misplaced 'em," Gladdie consoled him. "Maybe you put 'em someplace different than you thought."

Drusie was sure June wouldn't be interested in cuff links. She hadn't been near Archie any more than necessary ever since the incident with the dresses, and Drusie had become convinced that June had given up on Archie.

"I just hope they turn up," Archie said.

"They cost a pretty penny, didn't they?" Gladdie asked.

"You shred it, wheat. And I'd better not catch anybody wearing them."

"I ain't wearin' your cuff links." Gladdie held his arms out for Archie to see. "I cain't afford shirts with no fancy cuffs. All my shirts button."

"I wasn't thinking of you, genius. You don't have a criminal bone in your body. But if you get any ideas about who might have made off with my cuff links, let me know." He made a quick exit.

"He sure is out of sorts about them cuff links," Drusie noticed.

"I would be, too, if I lost something that valuable. You don't think anybody made off with 'em, do you?"

"I sure hope not. If they did, they're in a heap of trouble with Archie."

⁂

Two nights later, they were getting ready to perform again when Drusie noticed that the woman in fur was back. She couldn't seem to take her gaze from Elmer. He caught the lady's eye once or twice during the performance as he played the fiddle and played the straight man for a few rehearsed jokes.

So the mystery woman does have a reason to be here!

Concentrating on the music, Drusie didn't have time to ponder anyone's romantic life except for that of each of the protagonists in her songs. But after the show, she hurried to the hole in the wall that passed for the dressing room she shared with Clara. All she wanted to do was change out of her sequined dress and into a plain skirt and simple cotton blouse so she could get back to the motel and sleep.

Just beyond her door, she noticed a couple hovering. Elmer and the mystery woman were in deep conversation. Drusie winked at him, but instead of a jovial smile and wink in return as she expected, Elmer looked shaken. The woman turned to peer at Drusie. Her mouth opened, giving her a stricken look, and she darted away. Drusie pretended not to notice that their behavior was strange. Yet moments later, as she changed her outfit, she couldn't help but wonder why the couple acted so distraught. Elmer wasn't married or entangled with any woman as far as she knew. Surely the mystery woman wasn't married. She hoped not. But why else would they have seemed upset at being spied?

Lord, if somethin' wrong is happenin' under our noses, please offer Elmer and this woman friend of his Your light to the right path. Show them their error and set them straight.

But what if she was wrong?

Lord, keep me from being a busybody. Amen.

Clara entered the dressing room.

"Hey, you're just in time to help me with this button that's so hard to reach."

Clara assisted Drusie. "You gotta be a contortionist to get dressed anymore. Once I get rich, I'm hirin' a maid. Then I won't have to do nothin' I don't wanna do."

"Like dress yourself?" Drusie slithered out of her costume.

"Maybe." Clara grinned. "As long as I can shop, I'll be happy." Clara turned so Drusie could help her slip out of her garment.

"You don't need a maid. You got me."

"Not for long," Clara quipped. "Gladdie will have you home and in a family way before you know it."

"Clara! Must you?" Drusie felt heat rise to her face.

Her sister laughed. "Hey, you missed signin' autographs."

"I ain't worried none about that. The fans that really want my John Hancock will sure enough catch us on our way to the motorcar."

"But you won't be wearin' your gown." She grabbed a hanger. "And I won't be, neither."

"You know I don't care nothing about wearin' no gown."

Drusie sighed and hung up her outfit.

"You seem mighty thoughtful tonight. What's wrong?" Clara asked. "Feelin' puny? I have to say, that bean soup I had for lunch didn't set well with me. I could use a glass of ginger ale to settle my stomach. You don't happen to have none, do you?"

"No." She took a stick of peppermint candy out of her purse. "Try this."

"Thanks. Well, if you ain't sick, then what's the matter?"

"Did I say anything's the matter?"

"You don't have to. This is me, Clara. Remember? I can see when you're slow."

"Oh, all right. Give me a sec." Drusie cracked open the door and peeped at the spot where she had seen Elmer and the mystery woman. Not locating them, she glanced around and saw no one in sight. The coast was clear.

"What's with the cloak and dagger stuff?" Clara hissed. "Who do you think you are, the Phantom?"

"No," Drusie responded in a loud whisper. She drew close to her sister. "I know it's none of my business, but I saw Elmer and that mystery woman in the fur coat, standin' by one of the dressin' room doors just now."

"So he knows her after all."

"Seems stranger he wouldn't wanna own up to it. It ain't like he's married."

Clara flitted her hand at Drusie. "Oh, you know how shy he is and how hard it is to have a private life around the band."

"True."

"If I was him, I'd be likely to keep it a secret, too. And I say good for him. He'd do good to land someone as pretty as that one is."

"Maybe. Maybe not. All I know is they acted awful strange when they saw that I was noticin' them. She shot out of there like a raccoon with a hound dog on its tail."

"Wonder why."

"I don't know. I just hope she ain't married or somethin'."

Clara opened the door wider to exit. "I hope not, too. I say he just wants everybody to mind their own business, that's all. But you're right. It sure ain't up to us to be busybodies about it."

Approaching, Archie interrupted. "What's none of our beeswax?"

Drusie held back a grimace. How did Archie always manage to run up on them right when they were talking about something important? "Nothin'."

"Aw, don't give me that. You two were talking about something. What's your story, morning glory?"

"We were just talkin' about Elmer's love life, that's all," Clara volunteered.

"What's the matter? Is he dizzy with a dame?"

"Oh, we might as well say. You won't let up until you know," Drusie said.

"That's right. If I ever decide to quit music, I could be a detective—a house peeper."

"We just noticed he was hangin' around the woman in the fur coat who comes to every show," Drusie elaborated. "I'm sure it's nothin'. Besides, I have somethin' more important to ask you. When are we going to end this tour? Soon?"

"End it? You can't mean that. You're doing so well."

"We do fine when the producers pay. Not so fine when they don't," Drusie noted.

"Yeah, well, I've taken care of that. Like I said before, from here on out, you don't sing until we get paid. And you'll be getting paid plenty over the next year."

"The next year?"

"Sure. Why are you acting so surprised? Your father signed you both to a two-year contract. You have to expect to work."

"But—but I had no idea I'd have to stay on the road that long. Gladdie and I will never marry at this rate."

"Sure you can. You can marry the next time you go home, in the church and everything. I'm not such a bad guy that I don't let my stars go home once in a while."

"But even if we did marry, what kind of life would that be for a newlywed couple?"

Archie shrugged. "If you love each other, you'll survive."

eleven

With so many people around them, Gladdie hadn't spent much time alone with Drusie on the tour. But even a few sweet moments in relative privacy were enough to brighten his day. When they did manage to break away to a diner for a cup of coffee, he held those moments close to his heart.

They had been to a lot of diners—with and without the other performers—since Gladdie joined the tour. At first, eating out had been a treat, but now the diners, food, and even waitresses all seemed to look the same.

Drusie sat across from him in a nondescript booth. They were surrounded by what had now become familiar scents of diner food—gravy, vegetables cooked in ham hock, grits with butter, and beef cooked fork tender. Still, he longed for one of his mother's home-cooked meals.

"I sure will be glad when this tour is over. I'm thinkin' we shouldn't wait until spring to get married." He leaned closer to her. "Hows about we try for New Year's Day?"

"New Year's Day?" Drusie's expression hinted at vague disappointment.

Had Gladdie not known her so well, her lack of enthusiasm would have left him crushed. He decided to sweeten the pot. "Remember that jewelry store we passed on the walk over here?"

"Sure. What about it?"

"I noticed a weddin' band with orange blossoms on it. That band would look mighty pretty on your ring finger."

A smile touched her pink lips. "Yes, it would. But not yet."

"I know. We have to wait until New Year's Day."

The pained expression returned to Drusie's face. "If we want a settled life at home in the mountains, we got to wait longer than that. I just found out that Archie signed us up for two years' worth of tourin'."

Gladdie gulped. "Two—two years?"

Drusie's lips drooped. "That's a powerful long time."

"But how did he manage to do that without you knowin' about it?"

"Pa signed for us."

"But I thought he understood that we wanted to marry soon, and he didn't even seem all that excited about you goin' on the road to start with," Gladdie protested. "Why do you think he signed you up for such a long time?"

Drusie sighed. "I think he thought it was best for Clara. And I'm sure he figured we would make more money that way in the long run. To his way of lookin' at life, he must have thought the longer contract offered us more security. He always was one to look into the future and not take any chances. 'A bird in the hand is better than two in the bush,' he always says. Anyway, I don't know for sure. But whatever he thought, it's done now."

Gladdie understood. As long as the sisters lived under his roof, their pa would see to their affairs. It would be that way even if the sisters lived to be a hundred. Sure, city gals with big ideas might rebel against their fathers taking charge, but not Drusie. Since the cards had been played, everyone involved would have to work within the confines of the deal.

"I know he thought he was doin' what was best for you." Gladdie patted her hand. "I reckon he was taken in by Archie's smooth talkin', too. You know he can be persuasive. So try not to blame your pa."

"I know it. I keep rememberin' God's commandment to

honor our parents. Pa's a good soul, but he can be a trial without even meanin' to. I know the Lord knows I don't mean nothin' disrespectful in that." She stared into her half-empty cup.

"I believe the Lord understands. I know I do." He shook his head. "That Archie. I imagine he wants to make as much money as he can while he can. After all, you always said you weren't plannin' to be with the group long. Do you still feel that way?"

"It's better with you here, but as long as we're on the road, I don't see how we can get married. Don't you care nothin' about our marriage plans?"

"I do. Why else would I be offerin' to buy you a weddin' band today? You know I do. I don't want to wait, either." He stirred two spoonfuls of sugar in his coffee.

"Archie did say we could get married now."

"Now? But I don't want our first year of marriage to be spent on the road."

"Me neither, but there ain't no other way without waitin'. Once the two years are up, I can make a home with you, Gladdie. A real home. Not just some slipshod, halfway doin's. I want to get up every morning, early, and put on a white starched apron and fry you up some eggs for breakfast. I want to greet you when you come home every night from work. I don't care if that work is loggin' or farmin' or clerkin' at the store. I just want to be there for you." Her eyes took on a dreamy look, like she was watching a romantic movie with Gloria Swanson playing the glamorous leading lady.

"That does sound wonderful. Too wonderful. And contract or no contract, I'm gonna get you out of it." He placed some change on the table and rose from his seat.

Drusie followed suit and talked to him as they walked. "No, you're not. We cain't go against Pa. And what about Clara? She's blossomed since bein' on the road. I cain't take that away from her. And even though I dream of livin' in Sunshine Holler, life on the road ain't all bad."

"I know. But you don't want to be on the road forever, right?" Gladdie held the door open for her as they exited the diner.

"Well, not forever."

"Then you have to think of your own feelin's and not just Clara's. I know you never think of yourself, and in a lot of ways, that's good. But now it's time to. You cain't be Clara's keeper forever. Like you said, she's blossomin'. She's got Archie lookin' after her so close that nobody can get near her. She'll be fine."

"I think so, too, but Pa will be powerful mad if he finds out I left her. I cain't do it, Gladdie. I've got to stick to it—for the whole time. Pa will never let me go back on his word." She walked quickly to keep up with Gladdie's stride, holding her wool coat close to herself.

"That's right. It's his word, not yours. I don't think much of that. I was just plannin' on helpin' the band out until we went home for Christmas. I ain't comin' back for two years. Even though you're right—in some ways, it's kinda fun amongst all that hard work." They passed the jewelry store where the little wedding band shone through the window. He noticed that Drusie glanced inside, and he wished the store could be their destination.

He slowed his pace. "I want to wait for you, but it's hard. I've waited for you for years, since we was young'uns, and I'm tired of waitin'. We said we'd get married in the next few months, and now that your pa has signed you up to be with Archie forever and a day, I just don't know what to do. We don't need all this money you're making—or I'm makin'—'cept maybe to save up for the future, which is a good idea, I reckon. But we're simple folk. We don't need much money to live. I can work the farm and split the profits with Pa. Or I'll go back to my job at the store, even if I cain't own it."

"You don't want to do neither of them things and you know it."

"I'm the man here," he snapped. "You let me worry about how to make the money."

She flinched as though he'd slapped her. Maybe his retort did hurt. But she was saying hurtful things, too.

"I'm leavin' the band today. And that's final."

She didn't answer. Had she given in that easily? He didn't think so. Her silence seemed ominous. What was happening in that quick mind of hers?

As they approached the motel where the band was staying, Buford waved at the young couple.

"What's the good word?" Gladdie asked as soon as they drew close enough so there was no need to shout.

"Not much. I'm looking for my money clip. Have you seen it?"

"No," they both said.

"That's too bad. I had over twenty dollars in it."

"Twenty dollars!" Drusie clapped her palm against the base of her neck. Her mouth dropped open.

Gladdie let out a whistle. "That's an awful lotta money to lose."

Buford nodded. "You said it. You know, a lot of valuables have turned up missin' lately. What do you make of it?"

"I don't much like it. What else has turned up missin'?" Gladdie asked.

"Archie's cuff links, remember? And my necklace," Drusie said.

Elmer approached and interrupted. "What's the news?"

"My money clip is missing," Buford informed him. "I don't reckon you've seen it, have you?"

"What would make you think I've seen it?"

"I'm askin' around," Buford said. "So much stuff has turned up missin'—a few dollars here and a few dollars there. Plus, one of the stage managers said he can't seem to locate his pocket watch."

"Is that so?" Drusie asked.

Buford nodded. "Turned up missin' just this mornin'. Seems mighty suspicious to me."

June and Betty joined them. "Say," Betty asked, "how come there's a party and nobody invited us?"

"Yeah," June added with mock derision.

"I wish we was havin' a party," Gladdie answered.

"We're tryin' to figure out who done took our stuff," Drusie elaborated.

"What stuff?" Betty asked.

As Buford explained, Gladdie glanced at June and noticed that her expression indicated she was as mystified as everyone else. Either she hadn't taken anything, or she could act even better than she could sing. Gladdie observed that Betty seemed stunned, too. He had a feeling Drusie's hunch about June being the thief was off. But if neither June nor her best friend and partner, Betty, knew anything about the missing items, who did?

Gladdie joined in the conversation. "I wonder who could be responsible. It could be almost anybody. We're around so many different people in so many unusual places, it will be almost impossible to find a thief."

"Unless he's in our midst," Buford said.

In his mind, Gladdie ran down the list of people he knew. "I wonder if it's that woman that keeps following us."

"You mean the woman wearin' the fur all the time?" Drusie asked.

"That's the one."

Elmer bristled. "Any woman wearin' a fur doesn't need to steal. Come on, Buford. I'll help you look for your money clip."

"Sure."

They walked away, and Drusie noticed that Elmer's steps were determined. "He sure seems upset," Drusie said.

"A little too upset about us suggestin' that woman, if you ask me," June remarked.

"I'll see if I can find anything. You girls wait here." Gladdie searched the automobiles parked on the patch of dirt that served as a parking lot. "I see Archie's car. He must be back from town. I'm goin' to meet with him now."

"And say what?" Drusie asked. "We ain't leavin' the tour."

"I know it. But I can give him a piece of my mind."

"I wish you wouldn't."

"Don't worry. I won't say anything we'll regret. And if I do, he can fire us."

Gladdie went to Archie's room and rapped on his door.

"Come on in." Archie stopped combing his hair when he saw Gladdie. "Oh, it's you." He motioned to the corner of the bed. "Siddown."

"I'll stand, thanks."

"Suit yourself. So did you have a nice break with your girl?"

Gladdie was in no mood for chitchat. "I have somethin' I need to tell you. I feel like you took advantage of Drusie real good, and I don't think much of that."

"Excuse me?"

"You know what I mean. She thought she was signed up for a year at the most. Never two years. That's forever."

"Not in show business. Why, that's just a start. I got plans for Drusie and Clara. Big plans. And you'll want to be there for the ride. You'll thank me later, Mr. Harmonica Player."

"I will, will I? Why, I have a mind to leave with Drusie tonight."

"Good luck with that. You're not their manager. Take it up with their pa if you don't like it. The deal is signed, sealed, and delivered. I have a carbon copy of the contract I can get out of my suitcase and show you right now if you don't believe me."

"Oh, I believe you. But I didn't sign anything. I'm doin' you a favor."

"You are—an expensive favor. But you're free to go. I can make do without you if I have to. But not Drusie. Or Clara. They're contracted to me, and they stay. Besides, the longer they stay on the road, the more famous they get. It's for their own good to stay."

"You mean for your own good."

Without warning, Elmer and Buford shadowed the door.

"What's the matter, boss?" Elmer asked. "We can hear you fightin' two doors down."

"This fight is almost done," Gladdie told them. "I have half a mind to tell you to keep your money, Archie."

He noticed Drusie and Clara loitered behind the men. Good. They could see he was serious. Gladdie reached into his pocket to search for the two dollars he liked to carry with him for emergencies. The rest of his money was back in his room. The amount seemed a small sacrifice to make a dramatic impact.

"Here you are. Drusie and I don't need you or your money!" He threw the dollars at his cousin. To his surprise, something clinked on the floor.

Archie gasped. He rushed to retrieve the shiny object. "Buford's money clip! And look—a twenty-dollar bill. What are you doing with this?" He glared at Gladdie.

Gladdie tensed. "I have no idea how that got there!"

Drusie spoke up. "You can believe him, Archie. I know Gladdie, and he's as honest as the day is long."

Gladdie threw her a quick smile.

"Must be a short day, then," Archie scoffed.

"How could you doubt Gladdie?" Drusie asked. "He's your cousin."

"He is, but I haven't seen much of him in years. Times are tough, and people change."

"Not Gladdie."

One of the roadies interrupted. "Of course you're going to take up for your boyfriend, Drusie. But we can't afford to have our things turning up missing." He looked at Archie. "What say we throw him out, Mr. Gordon?"

"It's Buford's money clip. Maybe we should see what he has to say about it," Drusie suggested.

"I'm running the show here. What I say goes," Archie responded. Then he nodded, but the motion was slow and bespoke sadness. "I never thought I'd see the day when I couldn't trust my own cousin. After all I've done for you, too."

"Wait!" Drusie protested.

Archie shook his head, glaring at Gladdie. "I've waited long enough to find out who the thief is around here. I would have given my eyeteeth for it not to be you."

"But this doesn't explain the items that were missing before Gladdie got here," Drusie pointed out. "Archie, I think you're too eager to solve this whodunit and too mad at Gladdie to see straight."

"Oh, I see straight, all right."

"If you were, you'd see that somebody's planted false evidence on me," Gladdie protested.

Archie chuckled. "You've been watching too many motion pictures."

"Maybe so, but I tell you, I ain't the one who took your stuff."

Archie eyed his cousin. "Are you planning on hiding behind your girlfriend's skirt and letting her make excuses for you?"

"No, I'm not hidin' anywhere. But I can see I'm no longer welcome here and everybody's wantin' to concoct any story they can to get rid of me. I know you don't believe I'm a thief."

"Now see here—" Archie protested.

"See here, nothin'. I'm leavin', that's what I'm doin'. I cain't stay where I'm not trusted."

"I don't blame you, Gladdie, but you gotta stay. You just gotta. All this will get cleared up. You'll see," Drusie objected.

Archie crossed his arms and surveyed his cousin. "You can walk to the bus station from here and catch a ride home."

Drusie tried to stop him. "But, Gladdie—"

"He's made up his mind, and if he doesn't want to be part of our show, so be it," Archie said. "I got enough problems without all this bickering. We've got a show to put on." He nodded to the band members. "Load on up. We've got no time to lose."

Gladdie tried to keep his face from displaying his distress. He had expected his own cousin to defend him and to respond to his threats by insisting that he stay. But clearly, Archie was too carried away by his emotions to see logic. The urge to argue struck him, but with Archie in such a foul mood, he knew there was no use. Even worse, he was parting from Drusie under a cloud.

Lord, part of this mess is my own fault. I shouldn't have been so stubborn and prideful. Now I'm about to lose everything I ever cared about. Please show me what to do.

"What's the holdup?" Archie interrupted Gladdie's thoughts. "You said you don't want to be part of our show, and the perfect excuse to get out fell right at your feet. So what's your complaint? Now scram."

Gladdie gave no answer except to go to his room and pack. Archie was hardly the voice of God, but for the time being, he offered the only direction he could hear.

twelve

Onstage during the matinee show, Drusie heard applause but didn't absorb her success. She noticed Clara basking in the spotlight as usual. Obviously, she had put the day's drama out of her mind. Drusie envied the way Clara flitted about from hour to hour, not worrying about anything.

"And which of you with taking thought can add to his stature one cubit?"

The Lord's advice from the book of Luke popped unbidden into her head. Perhaps instead of envying her sister, she should follow her example of not worrying.

Still, Gladdie had gone against her advice and had ended up yelling at his cousin and saying regretful things. She had a feeling if the men hadn't been so fired up, Gladdie never would have tossed money at him and Archie never would have accused him of thievery and thrown him out on his ear. But the clock couldn't be turned back. Gladdie had been thrown out on his ear, and she had no idea where he was. She prayed he was safe. Or maybe he had talked Archie out of forcing him to leave. What if he was still safe back at the motel or, even better, watching her perform from a place where she couldn't spy him? If he was, she could make up with him. But what if he wasn't? She did know one thing—the music didn't have nearly as much texture without Gladdie's harmonica. Archie had talked a big game about being able to find another harmonica player with a snap of his fingers, but no such talent had materialized.

None of this would have happened if she had just stayed

home. Drusie wished she could go back to the way things were, when all she had to think about, other than helping her mother put up vegetables and clean the house, was when she could be doing the same tasks as Mrs. Gladdie Gordon.

She watched Clara sing a solo of "See That My Grave Is Kept Green," a song she could perform well and which was always met with great applause. Clara would do just fine without her. At least she had prospered from their new situation. And from the looks of things, she had even found the love of her life in Archie.

Lord, I don't mean to be selfish, but did I have to lose everything so Clara could have everything? Help me to understand, and show me Thy will.

Clara's number ended, and they launched into "No Telephone in Heaven" before moving on to "Sunshine in the Mountain."

Drusie laughed and joked with her sister in a rehearsed act, performed so many times that she knew it better than her own name. For that she was grateful. Such familiarity gave her a sense of comfort, and the sounds of laughter and applause helped ease her mind, at least for a while.

As soon as they strummed the last note of their closing song, "Let the Church Roll On," Drusie took her bow and headed offstage. Archie caught her and made her linger to meet a few fans and sign autographs. Her favorite fans were the children. Little girls looked up at her as though she were a fairy-tale princess. If only that were true. She wondered if Cinderella ever got angry with Prince Charming.

As was expected of her, Drusie signed autographs until the crowd dissipated, but afterward she hurried to find Gladdie.

Outside the door, she almost bumped into Archie.

"Say, why are you making tracks?" he asked.

"I want to know where Gladdie is."

"You know where he is. He left, remember?"

"I wish you hadn't made him think he had to go." Noticing the night chill, she wrapped her arms around herself. "Both of you got way madder than you should have. I think you were too hasty."

"He's the one who decided to leave. Truth be told, I'm sorta sorry, but that's the way it goes."

"Maybe he's not too far from here. Maybe it ain't too late to tell him you've changed your mind."

"But I haven't. I realize you don't understand the ways of the world, as sheltered as you've been, but I can't afford to have discord on the tour. I'm in no mood to fight with you, either. So if you're smart, you'll drop the subject or I'll throw you off the tour, too. Clara can sing on her own."

Drusie knew he spoke the truth, but she also knew that Archie had taken a shine to her sister. No wonder he could act so brave about throwing her out.

Archie wasn't finished. "You may have saved some of your money, but it'll run out. When you can't find any food and you're out on your own, far away from home not knowing anyone, see who'll watch out for you then."

"People will know me as a singer. I'll find someone who can help me."

He ogled her, though his expression was devoid of passion. "You're a looker, but take away that sequined dress and you aren't any more special than any other broad on the street."

She wanted to tell Archie he couldn't scare her, but the look in his eyes told her she'd better not be too bold lest he keep a watch on her and foil the plans she had made while she'd strummed onstage. "Maybe you're right, Archie. What was I thinkin'?"

"You know I'm right." His posture relaxed.

"I'm off to bed."

"Don't you want to take dinner with the rest of us?"

She wanted to beg off but knew if she did, Archie would catch on that all still wasn't well. "Sure."

Dinner dragged, but Drusie maintained a happy face. She kept hoping against hope that Gladdie would show up at dinner, but as dessert arrived, she could no longer kid herself. He had left.

It was only hours later, after Clara was asleep, that she sneaked out into the night, determined to find Gladdie. She didn't pack much in her little bag, not even her sequined dresses. Where she was going, she wouldn't be needing them. Besides, Clara would be sure nothing happened to them. She would keep them safe for Drusie until she returned to fulfill the rest of her contract. She resolved to be gone as short a time as possible. After all, she couldn't go back on her father's word. That wouldn't be right.

The highway was lonely and dark, but she wasn't about to give up. Putting her thumb in the air with the boldness of the most hardened hobo, she walked and tried to hitch a ride back to her beloved mountain home. Once she got there, she would find Gladdie. She would convince him to return to the tour. Surely Archie would forgive him once they reunited. Then she and Gladdie could set their minds to thinking of how to prove the identity of the person who was really responsible for all the trouble.

❧

Gladdie stopped for a cup of coffee at a roadside diner somewhere in rural Lincoln County. He was grateful to find a diner of any description, since he'd seen nowhere else to eat for miles. He'd missed the last bus out of town, and since the town in question was nothing more than a signpost, he decided to hitchhike and get as far as he could before moving on to any new ideas. Except he had no new ideas, so he kept walking down the lonely road.

Money had never been in great supply for him, but his needs were simple. He had managed to save most of the money Archie had paid him to help on the tour. His guess was that he wouldn't see his last paycheck.

Upset that he would have to go home in defeat, without a job, and on the outs with a family member, Gladdie stared out the diner window. He thought about what a mess he'd made of his life, all because he thought Drusie could earn enough money to make his dream of owning a store come true. Then his dream went bust, and Drusie sang every night for strangers instead of living life at home with him, where she belonged.

Worse than anything else was that he left on bad terms with Drusie and he had no idea whether they'd ever make up. She'd been determined to keep to Archie's contract. Maybe she was right. And maybe she was right about wanting a more normal life than they could have on the road, with or without being married. Still, he couldn't help but be angry at her. Once again, she had chosen Clara and her happiness—and her obligation to her pa—over him. Maybe he should just let her rot. With stage lights as hot as they were, she'd spoil pretty fast.

His hardhearted thoughts upset him to the point that he couldn't eat his food, even though the grilled cheese sandwich—the cheapest entrée on the menu—tasted almost as good as his mother's. He knew why he was so angry at Drusie. He loved her too much.

Still watching the world go by, he noticed that every few minutes an automobile or truck passed, but otherwise no discernable activity occurred near the eating establishment. Gladdie wondered how they stayed in business. Then again, the dinner rush had long since passed.

An automobile turned into the patch of dirt in front of the diner. Gladdie watched as a grizzled old man disembarked from the driver's side. To his surprise, a young woman wearing a green wool coat emerged from the passenger side. The man's daughter, maybe?

He looked again and did a double take. *Drusie?*

What was she doing with a strange man out in the middle of nowhere? Unable to stop himself in spite of his earlier unkind thoughts toward her, he rose from his seat and rushed to greet her. He met her just in front of the door. "Drusie!"

She looked stunned. "Gladdie! What are you doin' here?"

The man who had brought Drusie intervened. "You know this here fella, young lady?"

"Yes, sir, I do."

"And everything's all right?" The man looked Gladdie up and down.

Drusie nodded. "I think so."

"I'll go on about my business, then, but I'll be nearby if you need me."

"Thank you, Mr. Davidson."

Gladdie shut the door behind them, and they watched the older man take a seat at the counter. Gladdie spoke in a low volume. "You sure make friends fast."

"Got to, when you're on your own. So what are you doin' here? I thought you was supposed to catch a bus."

"Couldn't. Missed it. What are you doin' here? I thought you'd told Archie you'd be singin' for him for the next two years."

"And I will. But first I had to be sure you were okay." She slipped into the booth. "And I really do want you to come back to the tour. Archie does, too, but he's too proud to admit it."

"Aw, Drusie."

"I know you was set up with that money clip. I think Elmer and that strange woman that hangs around with him have somethin' to do with everything that's missin', and I think we need to figure out how to prove it."

Gladdie grinned. "I'm glad you have faith in me."

"Of course I do."

He reached across the table and placed his hand on top of hers. "But how can I prove my innocence?"

"I don't hardly know. Cain't we put our heads together and think up a way? We've got some time if we ride back to where the tour is." A question occurred to Drusie. "So how did you get here if you missed the bus?"

"I hitched a ride with a farmer who dropped me off about a mile from here. I was wonderin' where I would stay the night, when I decided I'd just stay up and keep walkin'. Maybe someone else would be on the road, even if it's already past ten."

"Speaking of the time. . ." the only waitress, a plump redhead, interrupted. "Like I told your friend here, we're just about to close. We're open bright and early for breakfast tomorrow, though."

"Aw, cain't you spare her a little coffee? You got some left, don'tcha?" Gladdie asked. "I'll give you an extra good tip."

The waitress shrugged. "I reckon I can serve you, then. Only, you'll have to ignore me mopping the floor."

"I sure will." Drusie nodded toward the counter. "What about Mr. Davidson?"

She regarded the older man as though he were hardly visible. "Oh, him. He's like family. He's here all the time."

Gladdie fired off a question to Drusie. "So who is your friend?"

"Mr. Davidson? I'm mighty grateful to him for lettin' me have a ride. He said he can drop me off at a motel tonight not far from here. We were just stoppin' at this here diner for a pick-me-up. You know, maybe he'll let you ride with us. I don't see why not. There's plenty of room."

The waitress set down the bill. She stopped for a moment,

looking at Drusie. "Hey, wait a minute. I think I've seen you somewhere before."

Drusie blushed.

"Have you just moved here?"

"Uh, no."

The pink-clad woman shifted her weight to one leg and eyed Drusie. "I know I've seen you somewhere before."

Gladdie couldn't resist prodding. "Are you a music fan?"

Stars seemed to sparkle in the redhead's eyes. "I sure am." She gasped. "Are you a singer?"

"Well, just for a little band—the NC Mountain Girls."

The waitress gasped even louder. "The NC Mountain Girls! Why, I saw you just a couple of days ago, up at the high school."

"That's right. That was us."

The plump woman squinted her eyes and put her head closer to Drusie's face. "Why, you're Drusie, aren't you? Your sister's name is Clara."

"I see you were payin' attention."

"Well, how about that!" She hollered toward the kitchen. "Lookie here, Jake! We've got ourselves a bona fide celebrity right here in the diner."

"You don't say?" A slim man wearing a stained white-bibbed apron came out to stare at Drusie. "Which one of you is the celebrity?"

The redhead whapped him with her towel. "It's Drusie. Drusie of the NC Mountain Girls. Remember? We saw them the other night at the high school."

"Oh, that's right."

She turned so fast that Drusie thought red hair would go flying. "Don't mind him. That night was one of the few we took off work. Usually we try to keep the diner open every day except Sunday. As soon as your show was over, we ran back here to reopen so we could serve the after-show crowd."

"Now Miss Fields is a big singer, Cindy Lou," he said. "She don't care nothing about how we run our business."

"Oh," Drusie countered, "but I find it fascinatin'."

"Well, aren't you sweet?" Cindy Lou smiled. "Sweet as pie. Speaking of pie, hows about I see if I can find a nice big slice for you? You look like you could put on a few pounds, and it wouldn't hurt you none. You like apple?"

"Sure, apple's fine."

Gladdie resisted the urge to search his pocket to be sure he had extra change for pie.

Cindy Lou disappeared into the kitchen, with Jake following behind.

"Ain't they nice?" Drusie whispered.

"Uh, yeah. They sure seem to be impressed with you. They didn't even say nothin' about me playin' the harmonica in the background."

"Oh, I should have said somethin'. Where is my mind? I reckon I was too flustered to think."

Gladdie dismissed the notion with a quick wave of his hand. "I don't care nothin' about that. Everybody knows I'm helpin' out Archie. My face ain't even on the placards. But that waitress recognizin' you and goin' all into a tizzy just shows how big a celebrity you're gettin' to be. Archie can make you such a big star that nobody will even have to ask who you are. They'll know you by your picture in them celebrity magazines."

"Pshaw. I don't wanna be in no celebrity magazine. I think I'd rather be just plain old me."

Cindy Lou interrupted. "Here you go, sugar. And a slice for you, too, mister." She set a piece of pie in front of Gladdie.

"Uh, I don't need—"

"Now are you turning down my home-cooked pie? I hope

not, because I sure would be insulted if I thought that."

"Hows about me?" Mr. Davidson called. "Don't I get a piece of pie?"

"I can't give away the store, Frank." Cindy Lou shook her head. "He comes in here all the time. Hardly ever leaves a tip."

"I heard that. I won't leave no tip tonight, either, then."

"Fine. It's not like I'd notice, cheap as you are." Cindy Lou's teasing tone belied her criticism. Gladdie had the feeling if he himself lived close by, he'd come to this diner every chance he could.

thirteen

Mr. Davidson couldn't offer assistance since he planned to travel in the opposite direction. Even with Gladdie at her side, Drusie didn't like the idea of hitching a ride back from the diner, then trying to find the tour so late at night. Yet without an automobile of their own and with no bus station in sight, the couple didn't feel as though they had another choice.

"It's gonna be a long night," Drusie mused aloud. "If it warn't for Pa givin' his word that we'd sing for two years, I'd hightail it right back home and never look back."

"Don't worry. We'll pray together before we set off."

Drusie nodded.

Gladdie bowed his head. "Lord, keep us safe throughout this journey we're about to take, and help us be kind to others since we ain't in a good position right now. Mend discord, Father, wherever we may find it. And help Drusie and me remember we are a brother and sister in Christ so we can show the world Your heart. In the name of Jesus, amen."

"Amen," Drusie agreed.

Gladdie summoned Cindy Lou with a polite wave of his hand. "If you'd be so kind, we'd like our check, please."

"Check? No sir, it's on the house."

"That's mighty kind of you," Gladdie said, "but we cain't accept such generosity."

"Don't you worry. Tomorrow's customers will be glad I had to make some fresh pie." Cindy Lou winked.

"I thank you kindly," Gladdie said.

"Me, too," Drusie added. "That was some of the best apple

pie I ever ate. Reminds me of my ma's."

"Either you really like your ma's pie, or you're terrible homesick."

Drusie smiled. "Both."

She and Gladdie rose from their seats.

Wind whistled against the building. "It's awful cold. Are y'all walkin'?"

"Hitchin' a ride," Gladdie said.

"How far are you going tonight?" Cindy Lou asked.

"Oh, about twenty miles or so. Ever heard of a motel called Sleepy Time?"

"Sure have. But I can't let you hitch a ride in this cold and in the middle of the night like this!" Cindy Lou looked toward the kitchen and shouted, "Jake!"

"Yep!"

"Our singers need a ride to the Sleepy Time Motor Inn."

Jake emerged, wiping his hands on an apron soiled with stains from the day's goodies. "All that way?"

"Now that's nothing," Cindy Lou said.

"Don't put your cook out on account of us," Gladdie protested.

"He's more than just a cook. He's my husband. And so if I want to get him to do something, it's my right, isn't it?"

"That don't mean I gotta do it," Jake pointed out, although his tone sounded good-natured.

Cindy Lou crossed her arms and shook her head, grinning. "I think you should take 'em where they need to go."

Jake shook his head back at her.

Cindy Lou stopped grinning. "They're good Christian people. I know because I saw them praying just now. Not to mention Drusie can sing a gospel song sweeter than anything I ever heard. They need our help, and it's up to us to do our part."

"Well, all right." He took off his apron to reveal a blue shirt.

"Oh, now you're being too generous. I mean it," said Gladdie.

"Now you let us be the judge of that. Besides, we don't have enough room in our house to put you two up for the night, and there ain't no places to stay nearby. So we sort of have to take you." Cindy Lou winked again.

"Well, if you insist. But we'll go only if you'll let us give you a little gas money."

"You can work that out with Jake. He handles all our money. Now I'll go pack you a little something to snack on for the trip."

Drusie shook her head. "Kindness like that can only be part of God's help."

"We'll just have to be sure we do good turns for folks in the future when we get a chance. I'll start now." Gladdie made sure to leave enough money on the table to cover Jake's gas and to thank Cindy Lou for her kindness. Though she had made the offer with no strings attached, he thought her kindness should be rewarded.

&

Later, as they drove along the winding road in the dark, neither Jake nor Cindy Lou had much to say. That suited Gladdie. He was tired. He noticed that Drusie looked more than a little sluggish herself. Truly the day had been a trying one.

Jake pulled into the parking lot of the motel. "Here we are."

"I don't see none of the cars that belong to us," Drusie said.

"They must have gone ahead to the next place," Gladdie surmised. "Figures. Archie's always tryin' to make time on the road."

Gladdie snapped his fingers. "Wait! I think I heard Archie say somethin' about the next gig being in Southern Pines."

"We can get you there," Cindy Lou said.

Gladdie sent her a regretful smile and shook his head. "We

cain't ask you to drive us that far tonight. We can just stay at this here place. We can get two rooms for the night and figure out how to catch up with the band tomorrow."

A rectangular structure with only a few rooms, the establishment was nothing but a roadside stop, convenient for tourists passing through the state or for singers looking for a place to lay their heads until they had to move on to the next stop. Still, automobiles filled almost every spot of the dirt parking lot.

"Hope they've got some rooms left. I won't leave you kids stranded until I know you've got a place to sleep."

"Thank you, Jake."

Gladdie hopped out of the sedan and made his way to the motel office. The place was dark, with no sign of life. He noticed a dirt road and realized it led to a plain house nearby. "I wonder if that's where the manager lives." He waved to Jake, Cindy Lou, and Drusie, then hurried to the front door of the white frame house and knocked.

After a few moments, a man wearing a nightshirt and hat answered. "We're closed."

"I know, sir, but I'd be mighty grateful if you could spare me and my girl two rooms for the night. We'll be stranded if you cain't."

"Stranded, huh?" He tugged on his graying beard and peered into the darkness. "Hey, I think I recognize you. Were y'all with those musicians traveling through here?"

"Sure are. I play harmonica, but my girl's the star. She sings."

"Well, in that case, I suppose I might be able to see my way clear to helping you out. There aren't many other places in these parts for you to stay at, so it's a good thing I answered the door. Don't always."

"Yes, sir."

"And by the way, you two are lucky I've got two rooms left. I wouldn't rent an unmarried couple just one."

"I don't call that luck, sir. I call it God's provision. And I wouldn't accept just one room for the two of us, either."

The older man's expression softened. "In that case, I don't mind so much having to get up in the middle of the night. Hold on a minute and let me get on some clothes."

Gladdie waited in the cold only a short time before the proprietor emerged and led him to the office. Gladdie detoured to the automobile and summoned Drusie. "We've got two rooms for the night. You can leave us in good conscience, Jake. We're mighty obliged to ya."

"My pleasure."

&.

Even though she'd been dog tired when her head hit the pillow, Drusie didn't sleep well. The metallic smell of steam heat mixed with stale perfume, cigarette smoke, dirt, mold, and body odor, as though previous occupants over the past thirty years had left their initials just as sure as they'd been carved on a sycamore tree. The sheets seemed clean, but they looked dingy. At home, her mother kept their sheets white and smelling of bleach, even if they were so thin a body could be seen right through them. Plaster walls, which she could discern thanks to the motel's lit sign, were once white but had yellowed from smoke and neglect.

The motel room was no worse than the band's usual digs. But it wasn't the sagging mattress that was keeping her awake; her thoughts were. It was the first night since they formed the band that Drusie had been away from Clara. She worried that her younger sister was all alone with no other woman she could call a friend or confidant. June hadn't pulled any fiery pranks since the dress incident, but then again, the jealous woman sensed that Drusie had caught on to her game. Without Drusie nearby, would June harass Clara? Drusie worried in spite of her earlier resolve. She realized that in her selfish pursuit of Gladdie, she had broken her promise to Pa that she would take care of her little sister.

Lord, forgive me. Please take care of Clara. And me and Gladdie, too.

❧

The next morning Gladdie didn't waste time before he knocked on the door to Drusie's room to awaken her. He wanted to catch up to Archie as soon as he could, and without a reliable mode of transportation available, he didn't think he could wait long lest they not catch the band before they moved on to the next town, wherever that might be.

"Comin'!" Her voice sounded chipper for first thing in the morning.

Gladdie smiled to himself. He looked forward to hearing that happy voice every morning for the rest of his life.

The door opened. Drusie stood before him, looking prettier than ever without her dark hair all dolled up and without a trace of face paint on her smooth skin. A crisp white collar peeked from underneath the top of her stylish green wool coat. He wanted to kiss her, but she barely threw him a glance. Clearly she was too preoccupied to think of anything beyond their journey.

"I'm ready, except I'd like a little breakfast. Do ya think there's anywhere to eat around these parts?"

"I saw a diner a few blocks from here when we passed by last night. But I don't know that we'd have time to get there and back before we have to check out. It's already past nine."

Drusie nodded. "We'll figure out somethin'."

A few moments later, Drusie and Gladdie soon stood before the office manager so they could check out.

"Where you young folks going after this? I don't see an automobile outside."

"We don't have an automobile, sir," Gladdie told him.

"You don't?" He scratched his head. "How did you get here?"

"We hitched a ride."

"Oh, I see." He handed Gladdie a few dollars in change. "Taking a bus somewhere?"

"I hope we can get to a bus station without too much trouble," Gladdie admitted. "We're tryin' to get to Southern Pines well before sundown."

"Southern Pines? Why, that shouldn't be any trouble at all. At least not for you. My wife is planning to go visit her sister in Fayetteville today. That's on the way."

"You—you are offerin' to let us ride with her?" Gladdie's voice sounded as bright as he felt. "That would be mighty kind of you, if you would. I'd be glad to give her some money for your gas."

The manager hesitated just a second. "That's all right. I remember what it was like to be young. Money's usually pretty tight. Fact, I know it's tight for you, hitching rides and staying here instead of some fancy place."

Gladdie and Drusie laughed.

"But 'Ain't We Got Fun?'" she asked, borrowing a song title.

"Living on love is a little easier when you're young than it is by the time you get to be my age," the manager mused. "Oh, by the way, I'm Oliver Dunbar. My wife's name is Bertie."

Gladdie introduced Drusie and himself in turn.

Mr. Dunbar tipped his head toward the closed door in the back of the office and shouted, "Bertie!"

From behind the door, Gladdie heard what sounded like the legs of a chair scraping against linoleum. He pictured the woman rising from behind a desk. Soon the door opened, and a wiry, gray-haired woman wearing rimless spectacles emerged. She was dressed in a pink outfit that looked better than the one his mother had for Sunday best. "You called?"

"This is Drusie and Gladdie. They stayed in our last two

rooms last night. They were with that band before."

"Which one?"

"Oh, you know, the tour that just came through here. Several bands touring together, I believe it was." Mr. Dunbar didn't bother to conceal his irritation.

"Drusie and I are part of the NC Mountain Girls," Gladdie offered.

Mrs. Dunbar looked down her nose at him. "Humph. You don't look much like a girl to me."

Gladdie forced a laugh. "Drusie here's the main singer. And her sister Clara sings, too. I just play harmonica."

"He plays harmonica real good," Drusie said.

"I'm sure he does." She shrugged. "We have a lot of bands that stay here. Sorry I didn't recognize you." She eyed them. "So you're the ones who woke us up?"

"Yes, ma'am," Gladdie apologized. "We're sorry."

"Happens all the time."

Mr. Dunbar nodded to Drusie and Gladdie as he kept his gaze on his wife. "They need a ride to Southern Pines."

Gladdie interrupted. "We can just get a ride to a bus stop if that suits you better, Mrs. Dunbar. Drusie and I don't want to trouble you no more than we have to."

"Now don't you worry," Mr. Dunbar said. "It's not out of her way." He looked at his wife. "You can take them along, can't you?"

Mrs. Dunbar assessed them as though they were tomatoes she considered purchasing at a farmers' market. Finally, she nodded. "You two don't look like criminals. And if my husband says you're all right, then you're fine by me."

Gladdie reckoned it took her long enough to decide that, but he opted not to make such a comment. After all, a free ride to the next stop was at stake. "I thank you mightily for your kindness, Mrs. Dunbar."

"I want to thank you, too," Drusie added.

She brushed off their gratitude. "Have you two had breakfast?"

"Now how do you think they've had breakfast if they don't have an automobile?" Mr. Dunbar snapped.

"I was just asking." Mrs. Dunbar's voice sounded testy. She turned her attention back to the young couple. "Can I fix you two a couple of ham biscuits?"

"That would be much appreciated," Drusie said.

"We would be mighty grateful, if it wouldn't be too much trouble," Gladdie added.

"No trouble at all. I've got to get on my wrap and fix your biscuits. Meet me out front in ten minutes."

Gladdie thanked Mr. Dunbar once more but hovered with Drusie near the door as they waited for their ride. Though not brutal, the weather was chilly enough that neither wanted to linger in the air any longer than necessary.

Ten minutes later, Mrs. Dunbar breezed to the front door and waved toward them in a motion to join her.

She had donned a surprising traveling ensemble. Gladdie had never bought a mink coat, but he was country enough to know real fur when he saw it. Her high-heeled shoes were well maintained and looked like they were made from real crocodile skin, as did her purse. Instead of the simple kind of hat his mother wore to church, Mrs. Dunbar wore a wide-brimmed hat tied down with a duster. In place of her spectacles, she wore heavy and unflattering old-fashioned goggles.

"I hope she can see with them things," he hissed to Drusie.

Mr. Dunbar quipped, "She can see just fine. Just uses her other glasses for reading."

Flushed with embarrassment at being overheard but feeling more confident thanks to the assurance all the same, Gladdie didn't respond except with a light wave and to open the door for Drusie to walk out ahead of him.

He hadn't meant to stare as they walked to her automobile, but apparently he had, as Mrs. Dunbar had a question for him.

"What you looking at, boy? Never seen a woman ready to hit the road?"

He made a point of looking at his shoes. "Uh, we don't dress so fancy where I come from."

Mrs. Dunbar chuckled. "I don't know that this is so fancy, but my father gave me this hat and duster on the very day I got my first automobile in the year 1922. Bought it with my own money, I did. I wasn't married then. Mr. Dunbar and I got married kind of late in life." She stared at a nearby tree but didn't appear to see it. She seemed instead to be somewhere else. "That car's long gone, but I've had these gifts from Daddy ever since. Goggles have seen some years of good use, too. No sense in throwing out anything that's perfectly usable, I say."

"Yes, ma'am." Gladdie thought about his motel room and realized that the same philosophy applied there as far as the Dunbars were concerned. Judging by their wear, the mattress and sheets hadn't been replaced since the year 1922, either.

Mrs. Dunbar inspected Drusie. "That feathered hat you got on won't last any time in the wind. You'd better take it off. I wish I had another duster to offer you, but I'm afraid I don't."

Gladdie looked up in time to see Drusie's eyes take on a concerned look. "You mean, there will be wind?"

"Of course there will be wind. I have a brand-spanking-new Chevrolet Phaeton five-passenger convertible. When my friends ride with me, nobody has to endure a rumble seat." Mrs. Dunbar led them to a dark green vehicle with its cream-colored top left in the down position. "Isn't this a beautiful automobile?"

Gladdie marveled at the large white walls on the tires. "She sure is, ma'am." He shot Drusie a look. Now he could see what Mr. Dunbar did with his money in lieu of spending it on making the motel look better and feel more comfortable.

If Mrs. Dunbar caught them exchanging glances, she didn't let on. "Mr. Dunbar gave Polly—that's what I named her, Polly—anyway, he gave Polly to me for my birthday last week. I'm not going to tell you which birthday it was, but I can say I've enjoyed celebrating my twenty-ninth year a number of times. Anyway, I haven't had much call to drive Polly yet. I'm excited about traveling along on the open highway." She patted the car. "You are, too, aren't you, Polly?"

Drusie shivered. "I don't mean any disrespect, Mrs. Dunbar, but ain't it a mite chilly to be drivin' with the automobile's top down?"

"Pshaw!" Mrs. Dunbar swished her hand at them. "I can't believe young people today are such weaklings. A good shot of brisk air will do you good."

Gladdie wanted to note that wind didn't whip right through fur like it did wool, but he decided he'd better not agitate the only person offering them a free ride to Southern Pines.

Mrs. Dunbar looked at her left hand as though she'd forgotten she held a paper sack. Without missing a beat, she gasped. "Oh, I almost forgot—your ham biscuits."

She handed Gladdie two biscuits and Drusie one. None of the biscuits held much in the way of meat, but they would do for a light breakfast. "Thank you," Gladdie said, along with Drusie. He proceeded to board the automobile.

"No, you don't." Mrs. Dunbar's voice cracked through the brisk air.

Gladdie stopped. "Don't what, ma'am?"

"Don't dare get in my automobile with food of any kind. I don't want ham grease all over my seats and floorboard."

Gladdie wanted to quip that the chance of their getting any grease from ham with her biscuits was slim, but he held his tongue.

"I'll wait while you two eat." She hopped behind the wheel and sat, looking as happy as anybody Gladdie had ever seen.

Standing in the cold to eat wasn't comfortable in the best of circumstances, but the dry biscuits made the catch-as-catch-can breakfast all the worse. Gladdie took small bites of his portion, wishing he had a glass of water, but getting a drink of any description wasn't convenient and would only delay the trip. Drusie ate slowly as well, apparently not enjoying her meal, either. Yet he knew she would never express a complaint about anyone's generosity.

"You enjoying your biscuits?" Mrs. Dunbar called from the front seat.

"We appreciate you for sharing your food with us," Drusie answered.

"Thank you mightily," Gladdie added.

Gladdie encountered a feeling of relief when Mrs. Dunbar didn't fish for compliments. At least he wouldn't have to figure out how to keep from telling her a fib.

"Here." Mrs. Dunbar handed them each a handkerchief. "Wipe off your hands."

They did, and without delaying a second longer than it took for them to position themselves in the backseat, Mrs. Dunbar started the engine, hit the gas pedal, and took off out of the dirt lot, setting the automobile on the road.

Gladdie watched Drusie hold on to her hat as the motor roared. Every time Mrs. Dunbar met another vehicle, she beeped the horn and waved. Obviously the act of driving invigorated her. She lifted her head high and stared straight ahead. Though he could only see her from the back, he could tell from the way her cheeks puffed out that a little smile decorated her face.

Gladdie noticed Drusie shivering, so he put his arm around her. Holding on to her hat, she snuggled closely to him.

Gladdie mused that the scene would feel romantic except that they were both freezing.

"I grew up in New England," Mrs. Dunbar yelled to them. "This is such mild weather. Hardly ever get a decent snow around these parts. Sure do miss the snow."

The last thing Gladdie wanted to see was snow. "Yes, ma'am!"

She glanced at them in the rearview mirror. "When do you kids plan to get married?"

Gladdie missed what she asked and responded to her mutterings. "I'm sorry, ma'am?"

"You didn't hear me, eh? That's just like a man."

"I'm sorry. I really didn't hear you."

She shouted louder. "I said, when do you plan to marry Drusie?"

"Uh, maybe you should ask her," Gladdie shouted.

She swerved to avoid a cat in the road. Gladdie held on to the back of the front seat for dear life with his free hand, and Drusie held closely to him.

"If we ever get out of this automobile alive, we should get married right away," Gladdie whispered in Drusie's ear. "Pa always said life is short. Ours might be shorter than we thought."

Drusie giggled, and Gladdie tightened his grip on her.

The near miss with the cat didn't deter Mrs. Dunbar's interrogation. "That's not a firm answer. Don't you have a date, missy?"

"Not yet," Drusie answered.

Gladdie wondered if she meant that or if she was just being polite to Mrs. Dunbar.

"Well, you'd better get one." Mrs. Dunbar let go of the wheel with one hand and wagged her finger in Drusie's direction. "My first boyfriend escaped me by promising to get married. But he ran off before he kept his promise. Skunk!"

"I'm sorry," Drusie answered.

"I'll never let that happen to you." Gladdie nuzzled her neck, relieved that Drusie had taken the pressure off him—and his voice since shouting was straining it—to field questions.

"Stop it. You're tickling me," Drusie teased.

"Maybe if I'd let the skunk nuzzle me, I'd be married to him now," Mrs. Dunbar shouted, then switched topics. "So where did you say you need to go?"

Drusie looked at Gladdie, and he could see in her eyes she was tired of shouting. "Southern Pines," he yelled.

"What's in Southern Pines?"

"Hopefully my cousin. He's supposed to be at a concert tonight."

"A concert? What kind of music?"

"Mountain music."

"Oh, I should have figured, with you being called the NC Mountain Girls." Mrs. Dunbar scrunched her nose. "I don't mean no harm by it, but I don't know that I'd like that music very much. A bunch of hillbillies blowing into a jug? No thanks."

Gladdie opened his mouth to retort but stopped when he encountered Drusie's elbow in his rib cage.

"Everybody has different tastes," Drusie yelled. "That's why God gave us different kinds of music."

"I suppose you have a point. Not that you seem so much like hillbillies or anything. It's just that my tastes run more toward classical. So where is this hillbilly concert?"

Gladdie responded, "I don't rightly know."

"You don't know?" They had reached the edge of town, forcing Mrs. Dunbar to slow the automobile.

To his relief, now Gladdie could answer her without yelling quite so loudly. "We usually perform in high school auditoriums, but not always. Sometimes we perform in churches."

"I don't have all day to hunt. My sister doesn't like me to be late for lunch."

"We don't want to make you late. You can drop us off anywhere you like and we'll find our way."

"No, I won't, either. I can't leave the two of you stranded with that luggage. What did my husband get me into?"

Gladdie pointed to a street sign where someone had attached a piece of paper. "Say, that looks like an ad for the concert. Can you stop?"

Mrs. Dunbar brought the massive machine to a halt by the curb. "You want to get out and look?"

Gladdie nodded and leaped out of the car. He memorized the information on the sign before returning to the car.

"What did it say?" Drusie asked.

"It says we're supposed to be at Our Redeemer Church at eight tonight. Says it's a gospel concert."

Drusie nodded. "Those are my favorites."

"Mine, too," Gladdie agreed.

Mrs. Dunbar ignored their comments. "I know where that church is. Do you want to go this early? If the concert isn't until eight, I doubt anyone's there yet."

Gladdie eyed a diner and wondered how long it would take them to walk to the church. "How far is it from here?"

"A few blocks." Mrs. Dunbar studied the sign. "Say!" She turned and looked at Drusie, then to the sign, then back. "Is that your picture on that sign?"

Drusie blushed. "Sure is, ma'am. To tell the truth, I'm surprised my picture's still on the ad."

"I'm not," Gladdie noted. "It's only been two days, and even if it had been two months, Archie wouldn't want to spend the extra money printin' up new flyers until the old ones was gone."

"True."

"Two days since what?" Mrs. Dunbar asked.

"It's a long story," Gladdie answered.

"It always is, isn't it?" Mrs. Dunbar studied the ad. "Well, I'll be! Drusie, you really are a headliner, just like Gladdie said."

"Yes, ma'am."

"How about that? Sometimes show people tell tall tales, so I had my doubts you were much of a celebrity. But that really is you." She studied the ad again and looked back to her young female passenger. "Although I did have to look close to recognize you. I must say, the picture flatters you."

"I have on a right smart amount of face paint in that picture, ma'am."

The older woman studied Drusie. "Hmm. I see the difference. I suppose you don't look half bad at that. You should wear lip rouge all the time."

As Mrs. Dunbar searched her purse, Gladdie whispered in Drusie's ear. "I think you're prettier without it."

Drusie blushed and smiled.

Mrs. Dunbar handed Drusie a piece of paper. "Here. Let me have your autograph."

Gladdie held back laughter. Mrs. Dunbar had been snobby about their music until she realized Drusie was a lead singer in a popular band.

"I'm sorry about what I said earlier about your music," Mrs. Dunbar apologized as she took the paper from Drusie. "I really do prefer classical, and I think singing three hymns in church every Sunday is enough gospel music to endure for the week. But I should have kept my opinions about your hillbilly music to myself. Why, you don't look like hillbillies at all. Not much, anyway, I don't suppose."

"That's fine," Drusie answered with her usual sweet spirit. "Maybe now you'll give us—and our mountain music—a chance."

"Maybe I will." She looked at Gladdie. "I didn't see your picture on the placard."

"I'm not a member of the band, ma'am. At least, not anymore."

"Oh." She slipped the paper into her purse and snapped it shut. "Well, I wish you two lovebirds all the best. Maybe I will try to catch you in concert the next time you come to town."

"I hope you do," they said in unison.

As he watched Mrs. Dunbar drive off, Gladdie was almost sorry to see her go. But he hoped he would never have to take such a harrowing ride again.

fourteen

Drusie and Gladdie went into the diner and warmed up with coffee. They lingered but couldn't hold a booth forever, so they ventured outside, taking their time and moving with slow determination. With nothing better to do, they spent the afternoon window shopping. This was no small feat, since at his insistence Gladdie carried both of their suitcases. They paused in front of each storefront for a time, with Gladdie setting down their baggage at each stop.

Drusie could feel tension mixed with anticipation when they neared a jewelry store. Some of the rings boasted stones that were very big, much bigger than Drusie ever wanted to wear, no matter how famous she became or how many songs the band recorded. The more she got out in the world, the more she realized that all that mattered to her was Gladdie. Mrs. Dunbar had let her first love get away. Drusie didn't want that to happen to her.

They stared at mannequins dressed in the latest styles. Drusie couldn't help but dream of herself dressed in the rose-colored suit and matching hat displayed in one window. The man's dark blue suit next to it looked sharp, too. She imagined Gladdie turning heads in such an outfit. She longed for a night out, regardless of what she would be wearing. She missed the church socials and her friends back home. Life on the road didn't offer too many breaks for any of the band members. She guessed that some of the tension and backstage drama had much to do with everyone being plumb worn out.

"What do you think we should say to Archie when we see him?" Gladdie ventured.

Drusie didn't answer right away. "I don't know." She strolled to the next window and focused on yet another display. Natural mink fur trimmed a beige suit. She noticed that the fur was punctuated with darker brown hairs that gave it texture. Not that she cared, but studying it helped her to concentrate on thinking about how to get Gladdie back in Archie's good graces.

"I think the world and all of Archie, but he can be a vexation at times."

"And from the looks of things, we just might have him as a brother-in-law, too."

"Clara's that far gone, huh?"

"I'm afraid so. I would have rather seen her set her sights on a stronger Christian, but I cain't make decisions for her. Besides, I don't think she'll consent to marry him until he gets closer to the Lord."

"Wonder when that will be." Gladdie's voice was tinged with regret.

"Soon, I hope." She sighed. "He's made my sister happier than she's ever been. We all grew up together. You know what she's like. She's always loved attention, and she's never had a chance to wear pretty clothes, at least not the fancy clothes Archie puts us in to sing onstage."

"I wonder if your pa would mind if he could see you."

"I don't think he'd mind. Even under the spotlights, nobody can see through them. And I wouldn't agree to wear anything low cut. I'm glad Archie didn't insist."

"Well, you do sing gospel songs," Gladdie pointed out.

"True." Drusie sighed. "Archie has invested money in us. I feel kind of guilty about that, even though I do think he took advantage of us just a little bit." She looked at Gladdie, unable to hide her distress. "I'm sorry to have to say that about your cousin."

"How Archie behaves ain't your fault. No point in lyin' about it to spare my feelin's. I'm sorry things didn't turn out the way we thought they would."

"It's all my fault," Drusie said. "I didn't know what I was gettin' into when I first wanted to play for Archie. I just knew I liked to sing and that my friends and family thought I was right good. When Archie agreed, you could've knocked me over with a feather. I mean, it's one thing for your ma to say you sing good, but it's a horse of another color for a man like Archie to like what you do."

"I know it." Gladdie picked up their suitcases. By resuming a slow pace to the next window, he encouraged Drusie to keep moving. "Don't you never think you're no good at singin'. I think you can live the rest of your days out knowin' that people—all kinds of people—think you sing good. Even if all this turns out bad, you've had a chance not everybody gets. And that is to live out a dream that a whole lot of singers would've given their eyeteeth for." Gladdie set down their luggage.

Drusie peered into the hardware store window but didn't take much interest in a wheelbarrow and a sign promising that seed orders for spring planting would be taken starting January. "You're right. Archie did give me a chance not many girls ever get. I'll have to thank him for that, no matter what."

Tired of staring at the wheelbarrow, she edged away. Gladdie picked up their suitcases and they walked toward the corner, planning to stroll through the residential section. They had the address and knew the road would lead to the church where the bands were scheduled to perform that evening. The waitress at the diner had told them they'd have to pass through a few blocks of houses before they'd find a small white church on the corner of Fifth and Elm. Gladdie kept pace beside her.

Lord, thank You for sending us sunshine and not much of a breeze so we don't freeze to death.

Drusie noticed a large residence on a lawn that looked like it would take a lot of upkeep. Maybe being rich had its advantages, but Drusie couldn't imagine herself in charge of a big home like the one they were passing.

"You'd like a big house like that one day, wouldn't you?" Gladdie mused.

"Naw, I was thinkin' just the opposite. I reckon I'll always be a little mountain girl."

"That's why you're so popular singin'. People see you're genuine, and they like that. When you sing a song, they know you mean it."

"I'm glad you think that. Sometimes I wonder, I get so tired. I thought singin' would be an easy way to make some fast money. And I suppose in some ways, it is. I have grown to like performin' for the crowds." Drusie sighed. "But you know somethin'? Goin' here, there, and yonder with the band has taught me somethin' important. Entertainers are paid to make what they do look easy. They have to look like they're havin' the best time in the world, singin' their hearts out night after night after night. They have to make it look like they've only sang their songs once or twice, not a hundred times, so many times they're sick of every tune. Some nights, I wish I never had to hear a banjo play again. But until you fell out with Archie, I kept goin'. For Clara. And so we could have us a nice little nest egg."

"I'll always love you for that." He sent her the crooked grin she knew and loved.

"And I'll always love you, too." To keep from getting too sentimental in public, Drusie changed the subject. "There's the church."

"Sure looks like it. It should be unlocked. We can go into

the sanctuary and rest and pray."

"That's a fine idea. Hey, how are we gonna handle this situation with Archie? We've been together all day, and even with all our prayers, I don't sense a firm answer from the Lord on what to do about this, exactly. Have you?"

"No."

"We still ain't come up with a way to prove Elmer and that strange woman are to blame for all the missin' stuff. I reckon even our brains together are a mite puny."

Gladdie laughed. "Maybe so. But not as puny as all that. I've been thinkin', maybe it's not up to us to prove nothin'."

"Say what?"

"I know it sounds odd, but I mean it. I've been thinkin' and thinkin', and I just don't feel right about tryin' to prove anything about Elmer. I don't think it's my place, somehow."

A phrase from Romans popped into Drusie's head. " 'Vengeance is mine; I will repay, saith the Lord.'"

As they approached the church, Drusie's stomach tied itself into a knot when she noticed Archie's automobile parked out front in all its cream-colored glory. "They must be early."

"Must be. But I don't think that should keep us from prayin'." He stopped, and they took a moment to ask the Lord for the right words. As soon as they did, Drusie felt stronger. She sensed that Gladdie did, too.

The band was unpacking in the sanctuary. Archie was off by himself, talking with two men Gladdie hadn't seen before. He watched his cousin pat one on the shoulder and wondered who they were.

"Archie! I'm back!" Drusie called to him. She touched Gladdie's arm in silent instruction for him to hold back on his greeting, thinking it wiser for her to see Archie first since he was a little less angry with her than he was with Gladdie. At least, she hoped.

Archie didn't hesitate to turn his head toward the sound of her voice. He smiled and, excusing himself from his new companions, broke off from them and headed toward her. "Well, well, well! You decided to come back, I see. I knew you'd miss being onstage and all the accolades. Not to mention the pretty dresses. You made the right decision." He crossed his arms. "I hope you realize this means I'll be giving you a 10 percent pay cut. I can't have my canaries running off on me and then thinking they can just come back anytime without paying the piper—or should I say, the fiddler."

"I don't care nothin' about that. How's Clara?"

"She's swell. Why wouldn't she be? She's done a stand-up job without you."

"Oh." Drusie couldn't help but feel a touch of disappointment.

"Oh, all right," Archie admitted. "She bawled all night after the show." He shook his head and stared at the peak in the sanctuary.

Drusie felt Gladdie's presence nearby. "Hello, cuz."

Archie's posture became rigid, and his expression darkened. "What are you doing here?"

"I came here to be with Drusie." Gladdie pointed to his chest. "But I demand an apology."

"Sure. Have it your way," Archie said. "I'm sorry. There—is that enough?"

Gladdie looked as shocked as Drusie felt. "That was easy," Gladdie said.

"Too easy," Drusie said.

"Okay, I admit it. Your innocence was proven for you. June is missing her earrings. And I know one thing, if anybody had reason for taking her stuff, it was you. Or Clara, and she had plenty of people stand up for her saying she couldn't have taken them."

"That's a relief. I'd hate for Clara to be accused of wrongdoin', especially with me gone." Drusie knew how much Archie wanted Clara on the tour at any cost, but she refrained from expressing the sentiment.

Archie nodded and elaborated. "June was wearing them when you left, and they disappeared last night after the show." In an uncharacteristic motion, he stared at his wing-tipped shoes and shuffled his feet. "Truth be told, I knew you didn't take anything, Gladdie. I was just so steaming mad about everything that's happened that all I could see was red. I was looking for an excuse to throw you out, and I took it." He looked back at Gladdie. "So I guess I should say I'm sorry I flew off the handle last night. I do want you back in the band." He extended his hand. "Deal?"

Gladdie accepted his hand. "Deal. But if I'm ever accused of wrongdoin' again, I expect you to take up for me."

"Will do."

One of the men to whom Archie had been speaking interrupted. "Mr. Gordon, we're ready."

"Okay, go ahead." Archie introduced the men to Gladdie and Drusie as a duo, the Rustling Rangers.

The taller of the two stared at Drusie and snapped his fingers. "Hey! Aren't you one of the NC Mountain Girls?"

"Drusie Fields." She extended her hand, which the man accepted.

"Bill Richards, ma'am." He tipped his cowboy hat. "And this here's my partner and brother, Milton."

"Nice to meet you both."

"Uh, are you going to listen to us play?"

"I'd like to."

Milton let out a whistle. "I didn't know a celebrity would be listening to us audition." Milton and Drusie shook hands. "Now I think I might be a little nervous."

Drusie laughed. "I'm nothin' much. I'm just a mountain girl

who loves singin' and listenin' to good music just like anybody else."

Gladdie watched the exchange as he hovered in the background. The longer Drusie stayed a celebrity, the more he became accustomed to being shunted aside while Drusie accepted accolades. He was glad God hadn't made him a proud man. His pa never would have let his ma take over like that.

"Okay, enough booshwashing," Archie prodded. "I don't have all day. I've got a show to put on. Let's hear you."

"Sure thing." Bill nodded to his partner, and the Rustling Rangers struck a few chords of an old mountain hymn. Even though the playing caused the people in the sanctuary to stop and listen, their expressions approving, the men had sung only half a verse before Archie stopped them.

"What else have you got?"

Both men stopped playing mid-note and shook a bit. Bill was the first to regain his composure. "We got plenty." He mumbled something to Milton, and they began a song Gladdie had never heard with a melody that possessed a bluegrass feel. Archie let them sing up to the chorus before getting them to move on to the next tune. The dance went on through several songs, including two hymns. Through it all, Archie didn't show any reaction.

"Well?" Bill asked, clutching his fiddle as though it might break if Archie's opinion wasn't favorable.

Archie looked at Drusie and Gladdie. "What do y'all think?"

"I think they're good," Drusie said. "Better than good—I think they're grand."

"Good enough to cut a record?"

"More than good enough."

Archie looked at the men, whose faces had relaxed with relief. "Are you from around these parts?"

"No. We're from Clarksville, Virginia. We drove to Raleigh

to see you, but the studio was shut tight as a drum," Bill explained. "We waited until the next day, and then finally one of your men, Harry, opened up shop. He listened to us and said we were good, but he couldn't help us. You had to make the decision. But he said you were on the road and wouldn't be back for a spell. He told us you'd be here tonight. I don't 'spect he thought we'd drive all this way to find you, but we did. I appreciate you for giving us a chance like this, Mr. Gordon."

"Persistence can often outweigh talent, although you've got plenty of both," Archie said. "If you had said this was your hometown, I'd have guessed that everyone would be rooting for you strong. But since no one around here knows you—that's right, isn't it? No one knows you?"

"That's right."

"Well, I see you went to a lot of trouble to secure an audition with me," Archie said, "and that means a lot. That shows me that you have the determination to make it in this business. So I have a proposition for you. Will you play a few gospel songs before the NC Mountain Girls go on tonight and see how you do with the audience? If they like you, I'd be leaning toward offering you a chance to record."

"We'll take that chance, Mr. Gordon!" Bill exclaimed. "Thank you mightily. We appreciate it an awful lot."

"That's fine. You two fellows go ahead and practice. Showtime's at eight sharp. I don't like to keep my audience waiting."

"Yes, sir, Mr. Gordon. We won't keep them waiting. No, sir." The men hurried out of the sanctuary.

"Looks like you've made someone else's dreams come true," Drusie remarked.

"That's what I do. I make dreams come true." Archie's smile bespoke the smugness of control.

"You will let them make a record if the audience likes them, won't you, Archie?" Gladdie asked.

"Of course I will. They don't realize it, but I'd give them a contract anyway. I figured I might as well give the audience a bonus. Publicity will do everyone good." Archie winked. "Now you better get hopping, Drusie, and get that dress on. Your blue one, since this is a church. Showtime will be here before you know it."

Drusie found Clara in the dressing room, standing in front of the mirror, making sure every hair was in place. "Clara?"

She spun to face Drusie and put her hand on her chest. "Don't scare me like that!" Her eyes widened. "What are you doin' here?"

"I'm here to fulfill my contract. Is that okay with you?"

"Okay? It's better than okay!" Clara ran toward her for a hug. "I'm so glad you came back. Don't you ever leave me again without sayin' somethin' first. So what happened?"

Drusie shared the story of her adventure.

"That's really somethin'." Clara shook her head. "I'm so glad you're safe and sound and back here where you belong."

The sisters embraced once again, and Drusie's heart felt warmer.

ﮎ

Archie proved to be right. Time did fly, and the show went even better than they expected. For churches, Archie always suspended his usual rule of advance payment, opting for donations. As promised, a love offering was taken, and Gladdie helped man the booth where they sold copies of their recordings.

Drusie came up to them after signing autographs.

"How did you like that? All those people loving you?" Archie asked.

"I always enjoy when people like my music."

"Keen. We're just getting started making real money." Archie rubbed his palms together. "This is going to be some kind of take tonight."

Gladdie interrupted. "I don't know. These people probably don't have a lot of money. I just hope they enjoyed the music."

"That's why you're not a businessman, Gladdie. You have no acumen for money."

"Whatever you say, Archie."

The promoter tapped Archie on the shoulder. "Boss, I've got to speak with you."

Gladdie didn't like the look on his face, and judging from Archie's concerned expression, he didn't, either.

"What's the matter, Earl?"

"The love offering. It's gone. All of it."

fifteen

Stunned by the news of the missing money, Drusie, along with everyone else, looked at Archie. He looked even more shocked than when they found the burned dress.

"What do you mean, the love offering's gone? That just can't be," Archie said.

"It can be, and it is. I'm sorry." The deacon's voice was low in volume.

Drusie glanced at Gladdie, who stood beside her. Upset, she instinctively reached for him. He clasped her hand in his and squeezed it in a way that gave her comfort.

Archie wasn't so easy to console. "Did anybody ask the head deacon about this?"

"Yes, and he said he gave the money to a brown-haired woman who said she was with you."

Drusie couldn't help but pounce on the description. "Was she wearin' fur?"

"Fur? Not at the time, no."

"Oh." Drusie felt a little foolish.

"But she did have on a red dress that looked like somethin' you'd wear to a nightclub instead of a church, and she was tall."

"That sounds like her," Gladdie mumbled.

"Sounds like who?" Archie asked.

"The woman who's always around Elmer."

Archie groaned. "I hate to say it, but that does sound like her. But we can't be sure. I sure hope it's not her. Elmer's been with me a long time. I trust him like a brother. I'd hate to think he's gotten himself dizzy with a dame that isn't walking the straight and narrow." He snapped his fingers. "Maybe somebody in the audience took it. Yeah, that's it."

"I'd like to think a stranger made off with the money, but I doubt it. Remember, we did put on a gospel concert tonight, and I imagine we attracted mainly church people," Gladdie said. "Besides, I didn't see nobody actin' suspicious anytime after the offerin' was taken."

"And even if we could question anybody," Archie pointed out, "they've all gone home now. We'd never find them."

One of the older deacons approached. "I'm really sorry this happened, Mr. Gordon. I'm embarrassed that something like this could happen at our church. We have gospel groups singing here all the time, and this is the first time this has happened."

"I believe you. But can you help us? Can you describe the woman you gave the money to, other than the fact she was tall, wearing a fancy red dress, and had brown hair?"

He thought for a moment. "Well, I can tell you that as soon as she took the money, she stuffed it in her purse and put on a fur coat."

"A long, dark fur?" Archie's voice rang with defeat.

He nodded. "It was the only fur I saw here tonight. She stuck out like a sore thumb, because most of the people around these parts can't afford such luxury. I'm sorry, Mr. Gordon. I guess I should have asked more questions," the deacon apologized. "But I mean, she was dressed so nice, like a motion picture star, and wearing that fur and all. She acted like she was in charge, so I assumed she was since she said she was with the band. Why, I thought maybe she might have been your wife."

"It's not your fault. We'll get the money as soon as the band member she hangs out with shows up. I'm sure it's all a mistake. He'll set things right," Archie answered.

"Hey, I heard the money's missing," one of the stagehands complained, approaching from behind. "If this keeps on, I'll be going in the hole working for you, Arch."

Mutters of discontent rippled through the tour members.

Archie waved his hands in a soothing motion. "Hold on. We'll get our money back as soon as we find Elmer. Go on now and let's get the gang together, and then we can all get paid and sleep better tonight."

"I hope so," June sniped.

Soon the band members were gathered, except for one.

"Where's Elmer?" Gladdie asked.

"I don't know. I couldn't find him," Archie admitted.

"I don't know where he is, either," Gladdie said. "I hollered into the men's dressing room, and I thought everyone would show up like usual. I don't know why he wouldn't."

"Maybe he's with his girl," Clara guessed.

"I wish he'd show up." Archie's tone indicated his impatience. "Now that he's not here for the meeting, I have a feeling something's rotten in Denmark. Does anybody around here know where he is?" Archie scanned the faces around him.

No one had a good answer.

"I remember seein' that woman who always hangs around him," June noted.

"I saw her, too," Betty said. "Boy, oh boy, that coat she had on was sure swell."

"Sure was," June agreed. "She was in the audience tonight. Second row center, as usual. I can't help but wonder if she's got something to do with it."

"Could be," Gladdie said. "When they're together, somethin' always turns up missin'. I'm thinkin' back, and every time a trinket or money gets lost, that woman has been with him that day."

Drusie thought for a moment. "You know somethin', you're right. I always was more than a mite suspicious of that woman, but I didn't have her pegged as a thief."

Waves of agreement sounded among the tour members.

"Of course I'm right," Gladdie joked before turning serious. "Only this time, I wish I was wrong."

"Maybe you're still wrong," Archie said. "But if you're not, don't worry. Elmer's still around here somewhere and we'll expose him. If he's guilty, I suspect that for now he's playing it cool and not running since he's a band member."

"True," Betty said, "but he should have shown up to the meeting if he didn't want us to suspect anything."

"You've got a point. Let's go see if we can find him and his girlfriend. Gladdie, you look inside. I'll see what I can find out in the church yard." Archie nodded to the women. "Clara and Drusie, Betty and June, you split up into pairs and look at all the places that just the women have access to and see if you can spot the dame."

"Sure thing," they all agreed.

"Maybe we should split up one by one and cover more ground that way," Drusie suggested.

"I wouldn't," Clara said. "What if she's got a gun?"

"A gun? I hadn't thought of that." Drusie's throat grew dry. She swallowed, but it didn't help much. *Heavenly Father, please don't let anyone get harmed in all this mess.*

"Be careful," Gladdie whispered in her ear.

"You, too."

Drusie and her sister looked through the church but didn't see the fur-clad woman. "She's a slick one," Drusie said, surrendering the search after exploring every Sunday school room that had been used by the women to change clothes.

"We cain't give up. She's got to be here somewhere."

"No, she doesn't. She may be long gone by now. I would be if I was her."

"But she cain't be far from Elmer, and he's due to play again with us tomorrow night."

"True," Drusie conceded.

Without warning, they heard a man shout in the sanctuary. "Stop right there! We've got you surrounded."

Drusie rushed up narrow wooden steps, with Clara following right behind her. They reached the top of the stairs just in time to see Elmer rushing out of the church. Gladdie ran behind him. Drusie and Clara ran to the entrance. They watched as Gladdie caught up to Elmer.

"Hey, what's all the fuss about?" Drusie heard Elmer say.

The men stood in a huddle and talked. Drusie noticed Elmer's facial expression change from disbelief to anger, then sorrow.

Gladdie broke away from them and approached the sisters. "Looks like that woman took Elmer for a ride. He thought she was interested in him, but apparently she had planned this all along."

"What?" Clara and Drusie said at once.

The shake of Gladdie's head conveyed his sadness. "That's right. Elmer thinks she must have been the one who took all our things. I don't know that he's all that surprised. I reckon he's overheard people talking about his girl for quite some time and he didn't want to believe she could do anything wrong. But I can see how sorry he is. He told me now he understands why she didn't want anybody to know they were seeing each other. She had planned this big take all along, it seems."

"How sad." Clara's eyes misted.

"It is sad. His heart is broken."

Drusie took Gladdie's hand. "Oh, I'm so glad we didn't try to pin this all on Elmer. I would have felt just awful, even though that woman was connected to him."

"Me, too."

"At least they know it warn't us."

"Yep," Gladdie agreed. "At least some of us are havin' a happy endin'."

sixteen

The next day, everyone was anxious for news. Drusie longed for the return of her little gold necklace, especially since it was worth much more to her in sentiment than it would ever bring in money. She had a feeling the woman had sold everything long ago.

"No luck, Drusie," Archie told her. "They did catch her, though. She was trying to get as far away from here as she could—with another man, to boot."

"Poor Elmer," Drusie couldn't help but say.

"I know it. And poor us. She pawned everything. Even if she had saved the tickets, we don't have time to go find everybody's stuff. I can't even take a break long enough to find my cuff links. They didn't hold any sentimental value. I left my father's watch at home. That's the only jewelry that means anything to me. As for the cuff links, well, it's a good thing I was able to buy another pair almost identical to the ones that were stolen." Archie held out an arm and showed them a shiny cuff link of gold inlaid with mother-of-pearl.

"Lucky you," Drusie said without much enthusiasm.

Archie shook his head. "I'm sorry you got a tough break, kids."

"I've got all the time in the world. I still want to find my necklace," Drusie countered.

Archie's sympathy proved temporal. "You might want to, but you won't be able to. You don't have time. You're still under contract to me."

"And so is Elmer?" she couldn't help but ask.

"And so is Elmer. He was a dupe. He's learned his lesson about trusting a pretty face too soon."

Drusie remained silent. She could imagine the hold the woman in fur had on Elmer.

"This has just been too much excitement. I don't know what I would have done if you hadn't been here, Drusie." Clara embraced her sister. "I'm so glad you're back for good! I missed you so much when you were gone."

Drusie laughed. "It warn't that long, but I missed you, too."

"I have a feelin' you're desperate enough to take me back, too, Archie." Though Gladdie's tone sounded light, Drusie knew he wasn't jesting.

Archie laughed. "I'm that desperate—if you'll come back, that is."

"Good. I got ya right where I want ya."

"You sound like a hardboiled gunsel in a gangster film," Archie replied. "Where's your Chicago typewriter?"

"I ain't no gunsel. I'm a G-man. And here's my Chicago typewriter." He pretended to spout off bullets at Archie with a Thompson machine gun.

Archie placed his heart on his chest and pretended to collapse.

"Boys!" Clara chastised. "We sing songs. We don't make gangster movies."

Drusie laughed, glad that the tension of the past few weeks was shattered and the easy camaraderie they once enjoyed had returned. "Okay, Gladdie, what's your big idea?"

"Archie's gonna love it." Gladdie rubbed his hands together. "How about you lettin' me manage the NC Mountain Girls? Then you can be free to go back to the studio and cut records with more acts. Maybe you can go on another tour yourself."

Archie didn't even contemplate the idea. "No can do, pal-ly. I'm not leaving Clara." Archie gazed at Clara with unmistakable love in his eyes. "But I tell you what. To make it up to you and Drusie for me flying off the handle and letting you go—and because you're a great harmonica player—not only can you stay with us for the rest of this tour, but you can have a job with me as long as you want."

"Well, it ain't as good as managin' the band. You really mean what you say, right?"

"Sure I do. I'm not in the habit of saying things I don't mean."

"I'll stay on one condition."

Archie raised his arms in mock surrender. "How many conditions have you got?"

Gladdie laughed. "Not so many. I want me and Drusie to marry soon—over the Christmas holiday. And now that Drusie's takin' a likin' to performin', and I have, too, I do want us to stay for a while. But I also want us to have enough time to have a home life while Drusie keeps her contract with you."

"You want to have your cake and eat it, too," Archie said.

Gladdie crossed his arms. "Yep."

"You drive a hard bargain. I'm proud of you, Gladdie." Archie emphasized his sentiment with a pat on Gladdie's back. "I think you've finally learned how to be a good businessman."

"What do you think of that idea, Clara?" Drusie asked, even though she could guess the answer. Clara's face looked rapt with anticipation. She didn't want to leave the music industry—or Archie. Gladdie's solution was perfect.

"What do I think?" Clara's eyes widened. "Why, I didn't know my opinion counted for nothin'."

"I don't know why you'd say that. You're one of the stars," Archie noted.

"I don't need to be the star of the show. I like singin' with my sister better."

Drusie sniffled, trying to hold back her emotion. She never

expected Clara, who loved attention more than anything else, to say that she'd rather share the spotlight with her than keep the accolades of audiences to herself. Perhaps the worldliness of playing music for money hadn't gotten to her little sister as much as she suspected. *Thank You, Lord, for being there for Clara when I was gone.*

"I have one more favor to ask you, Archie," Gladdie said.

Archie crossed his arms. "You're a good businessman, but I have my limits, even when it comes to my own cousin."

"I know. But we got this one comin' to us. Can we have a week off at Christmas instead of the two days you had planned for us? Drusie and I talked about gettin' married on New Year's Day."

Archie opened his mouth to protest.

Gladdie raised a palm to stop him. "You have to admit, even that doesn't leave much time for a honeymoon. And I know you don't have no concerts lined up that week. I wouldn't ask you to disappoint our payin' fans by cancelin' out on them. All you had for us to do was make another record. Cain't we do that later?"

"I don't know. We've got to strike while the iron is hot," Archie argued. "Do you have to get married over the holiday? Can't you get married anytime? There's a church in every town. Most of the time, you got your pick of places to get married in."

"But I want Ma and Pa and everybody else to be there," Drusie said. "Even though I don't need no fancy weddin'."

"Yeah," Gladdie agreed. "I want to go home so Drusie and I can be married by Preacher Lawson. He's been our pastor ever since I can remember, and I cain't imagine bein' married by anybody else."

"Me neither," Drusie concurred.

"Oh, all right. But only three days. We've got to cut more records now that everybody's excited about your songs and askin' about where to get the platters. You might be famous now, but they'll forget you all too soon if you disappoint them."

"But we ain't askin' for much time," Gladdie pointed out. "Just a couple of days."

"A couple of days? That's not much time to put on a big shindig worthy of celebrities." Archie ticked off the list on his fingers. "The music, flowers, getting your dress made, food, the invitations. . . I don't see how all that can be planned in such a short time."

"But I don't want nothin' like a celebrity would have," Drusie said. "I just want a simple day."

"I want what she wants," Gladdie agreed.

Archie lifted his palms in surrender. "Okay, kids. It's your day."

epilogue

As planned, the wedding took place on New Year's Day at the little church in Sunshine Hollow where the Fields family had worshiped for several generations. Pastor Lawson officiated at the ceremony. Gray clouds concealed the sun but not enough to threaten rain or snow. Friends and family surrounded Drusie and Gladdie. Drusie never remembered being happier.

Just as the tour ended, Archie had taken them to a fine store in Raleigh so they could choose dresses. Both men had traveled to a haberdashery down the street to be fitted for brand-new suits. She'd already seen Gladdie in his dark blue suit that made him appear dapper in a more subdued way than his lively stage garb. He looked like a model in a magazine ad aimed at a busy executive. She would have married him while he wore old dungarees, but she sure was glad he'd look dashing in their wedding photograph.

Drusie had bought a knee-length green dress for her wedding day, choosing a lovely shade that complemented her dark hair and fair skin, in honor of new beginnings and the season of Christmas.

"You've never looked lovelier," Clara told her.

Drusie didn't want to brag, but she knew her sister spoke the truth. She could feel warm happiness radiating from her face.

Remembering their family as they made ready for the wedding, Drusie and Gladdie had paid train fare for everyone to join them in Raleigh, where their parents and sisters chose apparel they'd wear as participants. Ma adored her mauve-colored dress with touches of lace. "Too good for me," she'd said, but her ecstatic expression told them otherwise. Pa looked dandy in his new suit, even though he did complain about having to wear a tie. Her sisters looked lovely in pink. As she gazed upon her family, Drusie smiled with so much pride her cheeks hurt.

Drusie and Gladdie waited as the wedding photographer set up a scene with a decorated archway to frame the newlyweds and their wedding party.

"Everything's so beautiful, Gladdie." Drusie let out a sigh.

Gladdie gazed into her eyes. "For the first time in my life, I have enough money to treat you right, and I'm gonna do it. Just you wait until you see where we're headed for our honeymoon."

"Where are we goin'?"

"I'll never tell." Gladdie grinned at his new sister-in-law and Archie. "Especially in front of these two."

Drusie grinned and swatted at him with her bouquet of six red roses that they had ordered from the new owners of Goode's store—relatives of the well-respected Simpsons—especially for her day. They came all the way from a florist in Greensboro.

"Now don't ruin your pretty flowers before we get our pictures taken," Clara teased.

"I know. But now I won't be able to think of anything else but tryin' to guess where we'll be goin' after this."

"Won't you tell her, Gladdie?" Clara prodded.

"Oh, all right. I'll tell you where we're goin'—Washington, D.C."

Drusie took in a breath. "All that way?"

"Yes, all that way. Don't you want to see the monuments?"

"Sure, but—but we don't have time."

Gladdie caught Archie's glance long enough to wink. "We do now. The time off is Archie's present to us."

"Yeah. But don't take too long."

"Always the businessman," Gladdie remarked.

"I don't care what you say; I cain't think of a better gift." Drusie sighed. "So much happiness today. We'll be back on the road all too soon."

"You regret becomin' a celebrity?" Archie asked.

Drusie thought for a moment. "Nope. Cain't say that I do."

"I'm glad to hear that," Archie said. "But I have to say, since being around you again, I remember the simple pleasures of home. And the love of God. I've forgotten Him lately, and I think it's time for me to get closer again."

Clara gasped. "Do you really mean that, Archie?"

"Sure do."

Clara beamed.

Drusie's heart warmed. With Archie's heart softening, maybe one day he would be her brother-in-law. She had a feeling Clara wouldn't mind one bit.

The photographer summoned Archie and Clara, along with the rest of the wedding party, for pictures.

Drusie watched everyone pose and smiled. "Just think of how much things have changed for us in so short a time."

"Ain't it the truth. I think it's been for the better," Gladdie observed.

"Me, too. Because of you and your grand ideas, I was able to take the music of home to other people, so they could enjoy what we know. I'll always be grateful to you for that."

"And I'll always be thankful to you for wantin' to sing so our future can be secure. I never imagined I'd be playin' harmonica in the band."

"Me, neither. I'm so glad Al is all better now and can play for Bill and Milton."

"Yep," Gladdie agreed. "Now Archie's runnin' two tours at once. It's unbelievable how his business keeps growin'."

"Unbelievable? I'm not so sure. Archie wants his bands to put on lots of gospel concerts, and the Lord blesses that, I think."

"I think so, too. And just look at how I thought my life was over when the Simpsons bought the store, but now everything is better than ever. The Lord always is full of surprises, isn't He?"

"Amen. Without Him, I couldn't have lasted a minute on the road. And He gave me my voice to start with."

Gladdie squeezed her. "That's what I love about you, Drusie. You never forget the real Source of life. You'll make me a fine wife forevermore. I can only pray that I'll be the husband you deserve."

"You'll be that and so much more, Mr. Gordon."

"I'll do my best, Mrs. Gordon."

"Mrs. Gordon. Imagine! I'll be Mrs. Gordon forever. Mrs. Gladdie Gordon." She sighed the way she always did when she watched one of her favorite motion pictures end happily.

Mr. Gladdie Gordon squeezed her shoulders, making her feel protected. "Do you think you'd ever be happy just livin' here with me and not singin' for the public?"

His query took her by surprise. "What does that mean?"

"I mean, will you leave tourin' behind when we have babies?"

"In a heartbeat!"

He beamed. "We'd better not say nothin' about our future plans to Archie. He won't like that much."

"Maybe he doesn't, but I do." Drusie lifted her mouth to Gladdie for a sweet kiss. When his lips met hers, she knew once and for all that they would be making beautiful music together for the rest of their lives.

A Letter To Our Readers

Dear Reader:

In order that we might better contribute to your reading enjoyment, we would appreciate your taking a few minutes to respond to the following questions. We welcome your comments and read each form and letter we receive. When completed, please return to the following:

Fiction Editor
Heartsong Presents
PO Box 719
Uhrichsville, Ohio 44683

1. Did you enjoy reading *The Music of Home* by Tamela Hancock Murray?
   ❏ Very much! I would like to see more books by this author!
   ❏ Moderately. I would have enjoyed it more if

   _____

   _____

   _____

2. Are you a member of **Heartsong Presents**? ❏ Yes ❏ No
   If no, where did you purchase this book? _____

   _____

3. How would you rate, on a scale from 1 (poor) to 5 (superior), the cover design? _____

4. On a scale from 1 (poor) to 10 (superior), please rate the following elements.

   ____ Heroine   ____ Plot
   ____ Hero   ____ Inspirational theme
   ____ Setting   ____ Secondary characters

5. These characters were special because? _____
_____
_____

6. How has this book inspired your life? _____
_____
_____

7. What settings would you like to see covered in future
   Heartsong Presents books? _____
_____
_____

8. What are some inspirational themes you would like to see
   treated in future books? _____
_____
_____

9. Would you be interested in reading other **Heartsong
   Presents** titles? ❑ Yes ❑ No

10. Please check your age range:
    ❑ Under 18   ❑ 18-24
    ❑ 25-34   ❑ 35-45
    ❑ 46-55   ❑ Over 55

Name _____
Occupation _____
Address _____
City, State, Zip_____

Louisiana
BRIDES

3 stories in 1

Devoted to their Louisiana bayou homes, three women find love while being pulled from their Cajun country.

Titles by author Kathleen Y'Barbo include: *Bayou Beginnings*, *Bayou Fever*, and *Bayou Secrets*.

Historical, paperback, 368 pages, 5³⁄₁₆" x 8"

Hearts♥ng

Any 12
Heartsong
Presents titles
for only
$27.00*

HISTORICAL ROMANCE IS CHEAPER BY THE DOZEN!

Buy any assortment of twelve *Heartsong Presents* titles and save 25% off of the already discounted price of $2.97 each!

*plus $3.00 shipping and handling per order and sales tax where applicable.
If outside the U.S. please call 740-922-7280 for shipping charges.

HEARTSONG PRESENTS TITLES AVAILABLE NOW:

___HP484 *The Heart Knows*, E. Bonner
___HP488 *Sonoran Sweetheart*, N. J. Farrier
___HP491 *An Unexpected Surprise*, R. Dow
___HP495 *With Healing in His Wings*, S. Krueger
___HP496 *Meet Me with a Promise*, J. A. Grote
___HP500 *Great Southland Gold*, M. Hawkins
___HP503 *Sonoran Secret*, N. J. Farrier
___HP507 *Trunk of Surprises*, D. Hunt
___HP511 *To Walk in Sunshine*, S. Laity
___HP512 *Precious Burdens*, C. M. Hake
___HP515 *Love Almost Lost*, I. B. Brand
___HP519 *Red River Bride*, C. Coble
___HP520 *The Flame Within*, P. Griffin
___HP523 *Raining Fire*, L. A. Coleman
___HP524 *Laney's Kiss*, T. V. Bateman
___HP531 *Lizzie*, L. Ford
___HP535 *Viking Honor*, D. Mindrup
___HP536 *Emily's Place*, T. V. Bateman
___HP539 *Two Hearts Wait*, F. Chrisman
___HP540 *Double Exposure*, S. Laity
___HP543 *Cora*, M. Colvin
___HP544 *A Light Among Shadows*, T. H. Murray
___HP547 *Maryelle*, L. Ford
___HP551 *Healing Heart*, R. Druten
___HP552 *The Vicar's Daughter*, K. Comeaux
___HP555 *But for Grace*, T. V. Bateman
___HP556 *Red Hills Stranger*, M. G. Chapman
___HP559 *Banjo's New Song*, R. Dow
___HP560 *Heart Appearances*, P. Griffin
___HP563 *Redeemed Hearts*, C. M. Hake
___HP567 *Summer Dream*, M. H. Flinkman
___HP568 *Loveswept*, T. H. Murray
___HP571 *Bayou Fever*, K. Y'Barbo
___HP575 *Kelly's Chance*, W. E. Brunstetter

___HP576 *Letters from the Enemy*, S. M. Warren
___HP579 *Grace*, L. Ford
___HP580 *Land of Promise*, C. Cox
___HP583 *Ramshackle Rose*, C. M. Hake
___HP584 *His Brother's Castoff*, L. N. Dooley
___HP587 *Lilly's Dream*, P. Darty
___HP588 *Torey's Prayer*, T. V. Bateman
___HP591 *Eliza*, M. Colvin
___HP592 *Refining Fire*, C. Cox
___HP599 *Double Deception*, L. Nelson Dooley
___HP600 *The Restoration*, C. M. Hake
___HP603 *A Whale of a Marriage*, D. Hunt
___HP604 *Irene*, L. Ford
___HP607 *Protecting Amy*, S. P. Davis
___HP608 *The Engagement*, K. Comeaux
___HP611 *Faithful Traitor*, J. Stengl
___HP612 *Michaela's Choice*, L. Harris
___HP615 *Gerda's Lawman*, L. N. Dooley
___HP616 *The Lady and the Cad*, T. H. Murray
___HP619 *Everlasting Hope*, T. V. Bateman
___HP620 *Basket of Secrets*, D. Hunt
___HP623 *A Place Called Home*, J. L. Barton
___HP624 *One Chance in a Million*, C. M. Hake
___HP627 *He Loves Me, He Loves Me Not*, R. Druten
___HP628 *Silent Heart*, B. Youree
___HP631 *Second Chance*, T. V. Bateman
___HP632 *Road to Forgiveness*, C. Cox
___HP635 *Hogtied*, L. A. Coleman
___HP636 *Renegade Husband*, D. Mills
___HP639 *Love's Denial*, T. H. Murray
___HP640 *Taking a Chance*, K. E. Hake
___HP643 *Escape to Sanctuary*, M. J. Conner
___HP644 *Making Amends*, J. L. Barton
___HP647 *Remember Me*, K. Comeaux
___HP648 *Last Chance*, C. M. Hake

(If ordering from this page, please remember to include it with the order form.)

Presents

Great Inspirational Romance at a Great Price!

Heartsong Presents books are inspirational romances in contemporary and historical settings, designed to give you an enjoyable, spirit-lifting reading experience. You can choose wonderfully written titles from some of today's best authors like Peggy Darty, Sally Laity, DiAnn Mills, Colleen L. Reece, Debra White Smith, and many others.

When ordering quantities less than twelve, above titles are $2.97 each.
Not all titles may be available at time of order.

HEARTSONG
PRESENTS

If you love Christian romance…

$10.⁹⁹

You'll love Heartsong Presents' inspiring and faith-filled romances by today's very best Christian authors. . .DiAnn Mills, Wanda E. Brunstetter, and Yvonne Lehman, to mention a few!

When you join Heartsong Presents, you'll enjoy four brand-new, mass market, 176-page books—two contemporary and two historical—that will build you up in your faith when you discover God's role in every relationship you read about!

Mass Market 176 Pages

Imagine. . .four new romances every four weeks—with men and women like you who long to meet the one God has chosen as the love of their lives…all for the low price of $10.99 postpaid.

To join, simply visit www.heartsong presents.com or complete the coupon below and mail it to the address provided.

✂ -

YES! Sign me up for Heartsong!

NEW MEMBERSHIPS WILL BE SHIPPED IMMEDIATELY!
Send no money now. We'll bill you only $10.99 postpaid with your first shipment of four books. Or for faster action, call 1-740-922-7280.

NAME _____

ADDRESS_____

CITY_____ STATE _____ ZIP _____

MAIL TO: HEARTSONG PRESENTS, P.O. Box 721, Uhrichsville, Ohio 44683
or sign up at **WWW.HEARTSONGPRESENTS.COM**